Until Johnny asked her to dance, Jean had not thought much about real boys at all. Boys were people who lived in the same neighborhood and went to the same school. Some of them were agreeable to talk to once in a while, and some were noisy nuisances. Certainly she had not thought of any of them as dancing partners. . . . It had been so much easier to dream about a boy on the television screen. With that boy she would be dancing lightly, gracefully. But with this boy, this real, live boy . . . well, it was all so different from her dreams.

BEVERLY CLEARY grew up in Portland, Oregon, and was graduated from the University of California at Berkeley and the School of Librarianship at the University of Washington at Seattle. She is the author of several award-winning books, including *Fifteen* and *The Luckiest Girl*, available in Laurel-Leaf editions. Mrs. Cleary currently lives in California with her husband.

JEAN
AND
JOHNNY

BEVERLY CLEARY

LAUREL-LEAF BOOKS bring together under a single imprint out-
standing works of fiction and nonfiction particularly suitable for
young adult readers, both in and out of the classroom. Charles
F. Reasoner, Professor Emeritus of Children's Literature and
Reading, New York University, is consultant to this series.

Published by
Dell Publishing Co., Inc.
1 Dag Hammarskjold Plaza
New York, New York 10017

Laurel-Leaf Library ® TM 766734, Dell Publishing Co., Inc.
YOUNG LOVE® is a trademark of DC COMICS INC.

ISBN: 0-440-94358-2

RL: 5.2

Reprinted by arrangement with
William Morrow & Company, Inc.
Printed in the United States of America
First Laurel-Leaf printing—January 1981
Seventh Laurel-Leaf printing—December 1982

JEAN
AND
JOHNNY

CHAPTER
1

"I have the funniest feeling," remarked Jean Jarrett, who was drying the supper dishes while her older sister Sue washed them. "I keep feeling as if something nice is going to happen."

"That's because this is the first night of Christmas vacation," answered Sue, rinsing a plate under the hot-water faucet and setting it in the dish drainer.

"I suppose so," agreed Jean dreamily, wishing that something nice really would happen. Lately life had lacked interesting ups and downs. Oh, there were little ups like watching Kip Laddish on television, just as there were little downs, too, like the plaid skirt she was wearing. Because she had forgotten to allow extra material for matching the plaid, she discovered, when the pieces of the skirt were sewed together, that the stripes were uneven at every seam. Little ups, little downs—how she wished she could replace them with big ups and downs that would make life exciting.

"What would you like to happen?" asked Sue.

"Oh, I don't know exactly," answered Jean. There was a speck of food on the plate she was wiping. She considered returning the plate to the dishwater for Sue to rewash, thought better of it, and polished off the speck with the dish towel. When it was her turn to wash dishes, she did not like to have dishes returned to her dishwater. "It would be nice to grow a couple more inches, and not have to wear glasses; but at fifteen I don't suppose that will happen. Maybe some-think like a cable arriving saying that a long-lost uncle has died and left us a fortune."

"That would be nice," agreed Sue. "He could be a terribly romantic figure, a family black sheep we had never even heard of, who had run away at the age of fourteen to Kenya or Bangkok and made his fortune in diamonds or teak or something."

"Or maybe it would be better if he had run away to the South Seas," elaborated Jean. "He could be a pearl king with crews of natives with knives in their teeth diving for oysters."

"Oh, well," said Sue. "How he got the fortune isn't important. What is important is that he died and left it to the Jarretts."

"It wouldn't even have to be a fortune," said Jean. "Just enough so we could have avocado in the salad every single day. And so I could walk into Northgate Apparel Shop just once and buy a plaid skirt with the stripes matched by somebody else."

Sue laughed. "I know what you mean. Money for little extra things. Oh, well," she said, with an airy wave of the dishcloth, "what are the material things in life? We have ingenuity."

Jean giggled. "Especially me. It takes real ingenuity to make such a terrible-looking skirt."

It was Sue who had the ingenuity. Right now she was wearing a skirt she had devised out of twelve red bandana handkerchiefs that she had bought at the dime store. With it she was wearing a white blouse she had made out of a remnant and trimmed with a yard of leftover rickrack. Jean remembered how Sue had schemed, rearranging her pattern several times, to get the blouse out of the short length of material. Even two years ago, when Sue was fifteen, she would have remembered to allow extra material for matching plaid. She was that kind of girl: she always knew what she wanted to do and then went about it in the right way.

Both girls were silent, each thinking of nice things they would like to have happen. She was right, Jean thought. Money for little extra things was a problem. House payments, life insurance, hospital insurance, money put aside for Sue's freshman year at the University next fall (their father said his girls were going to have a better start in life than he had had), a small check to help their grandmother in the East—all these seemed to consume Mr. Jarrett's pay check almost as soon as he received it. It would help if their father would allow them to earn money baby-sitting someplace besides the two houses next door, but he would not—not since the Friday night some strangers down the street had engaged Sue to stay with their children and had not come home until two-thirty in the morning. Mr. Jarrett, who was a mailman and had to report to the post office at six o'clock in the morning, said he lost too much sleep worrying about Sue in a strange house being responsible for strange children. Kids could get into the darnedest trouble, Mr. Jarrett said. He ought to know. He had seen enough of it in his nineteen years of delivering mail. If his girls were going to baby-sit, they had to do it close to home, where he knew what was going on. Unfortunately for Jean and Sue, their next-door neighbors did not often go out.

Or it would be nice, Jean reflected, if her mother won a really big prize in one of the contests she was always entering—a prize so big she could give up her Saturday job as a salesclerk in a shop called Fabrics, Etc., which sold remnants and mill ends of dress, drapery, and upholstery material.

"I know what would be nice," said Sue suddenly.

"What?" asked Jean, glancing at the clock. She must not get so carried away in daydreams that she missed Kip Laddish.

"To meet a boy." Sue's voice was wistful. "Not just any boy, but a really nice boy who liked me."

"Yes, that would be nice," agreed Jean seriously, because she understood that this time Sue was not joking. She was a little surprised at her sister's wish, because Sue had never been interested in the boys who seemed to like her. "But what about Cliff?" Jean asked. "He phoned you a couple of times, but you wouldn't go out with him."

Sue made a face. "He always said, 'Guess who this is?' and 'What are you doing next Saturday night?' without telling me what he wanted me to do. Besides, he would have bored me stiff. I am not interested in just any old boy."

"I suppose not." No boy, not even one who could be called any old boy, had ever telephoned Jean.

"Half a minute to seven. Almost time for your program," said Sue. "I'll finish up. We're practically through, anyway."

"Thanks a lot," said Jean gratefully, dropping her dish towel on the draining board. "I'll finish for you sometime."

At exactly seven o'clock Jean, her chin propped on her fists, was sitting on the hassock in the glow of the Christmas-tree lights in front of the portable television set, the biggest prize her mother had ever won in a contest. This was the moment Jean anticipated every week. And she knew that three doors down the street Elaine Mundy, her best friend, was sitting in front of her television set, too.

The commercial began. A pretty girl faced Jean and, while she smiled radiantly, wiggled her fingers in her soapy hair. The soap, by some magic, rose from her head in a glittering trail of bubbles that turned into a singing, dancing bottle of shampoo. Jean removed her glasses, held them up to the light, and flicked a speck of dust off one lens.

And then Kip Laddish was there in the living room singing straight to Jean. He was *so* good-looking. That checked sport coat, his trademark, made him look boyish because it was a bit too large, as if he expected to grow into it. And the way he sang. . . . He looked so serious, almost pleading, and then suddenly he would flash the most wonderful grin, that made Jean feel as if he were sharing a secret with her. It was almost as if he was saying, I know I don't sing very well, but we don't care, do we?

"Play like you love me . . ." Kip Laddish sang, and Jean sighed. She could hardly wait these next few months until he made his personal appearance in Northgate and she and Elaine went to see him. Without mentioning it to their families, the two girls had made up their minds, as soon as Elaine had spotted his schedule of appearances in a movie magazine, to see Kip Laddish in person and nothing, *nothing* was going to stop them. Elaine was giving Jean a ticket, or rather the promise of a ticket, for Christmas. They had even decided—if they did not lose their courage—to try to get his autograph.

"Play like you love me. . . ." It would be so wonderful if Jean could meet him. Of course that would never happen, but just supposing . . . just supposing she did happen to meet him. Just supposing when he came to Northgate he happened to drive down the street as she was walking along, and somehow he had got lost. Maybe he had stopped for a sandwich or something, and didn't know how to get back on the freeway . . . and there she was, walking along, minding her own business. . . .

The impatient rattle of a newspaper reminded Jean that she was not alone in the room with Kip Laddish. Her mother and father, as well as Dandy, the dog, were with her. She knew what was coming next.

"What a lot of silly girls see in that half-baked tenor is beyond me," said Mr. Jarrett.

Without taking her eyes from the screen, Jean carefully measured the impatience in his voice. Her trip to Kip Laddish's personal appearance would depend on her father, who, she had an uneasy feeling, might not think highly of such an expedition. "Please, Daddy," she said, knowing that she could not stop what he was going to say. His voice had already registered Impatience, well above Medium but not yet to Explosive. Her father, a kind and gentle man, rarely reached Explosive, but it was wise not to push him too far when he was tired from the rush of Christmas mail.

"He can't even sing," Mr. Jarrett went on. "He probably can't even read music and yet he has the nerve to stand up there in front of a television camera wearing a coat a tinhorn gambler would be ashamed to be seen in."

Jean knew there was some truth in what her father was saying—not about the coat, which was terribly smart although it might look peculiar to someone as old as her father, but about Kip Laddish's singing. It really was not very good, but that was one of the reasons all the girls liked him so much. It made him seem like a real person, someone a girl might happen to meet someday. A father could not be expected to understand this. "Lots of people like him. His records sell millions of copies," she said defensively, knowing that she risked running her father up from Medium to Explosive. If he reached Explosive, she would have to turn the set off.

Mr. Jarrett snorted an Almost Explosive snort. "If he earns so much money, why doesn't he spend some of it on a haircut?" he asked.

"Oh, Daddy, leave her alone. She'll get over it." Sue had entered the room and now spoke from the wisdom of her seventeen years. "Anyway, I sort of like him my-self."

"If the only boy we have to worry about is a boy on a television program, I won't complain," said Mr. Jar-rett. "We can put up with him once in a while if Jean enjoys him."

The rattle of the paper told Jean that her father had resumed his reading and she was free to dream through the rest of the program. Kip Laddish intro-duced his guest artist, a girl singer in a strapless eve-ning gown. He joked with her a few minutes before she disappeared to permit him to sing another song. Then the girl appeared in a different dress, a tight dress with the skirt slit up one side, and sang her song. Jean paid little attention to the tune, because she was won-dering how the girl managed to sit down in such a skirt. Time out for the tap-dancing bottle of shampoo again. Kip appeared with the girl, who this time was wearing a gown with a halter top and a short, full skirt—how *did* she manage to change in such a short time? Kip put his arm around her while they sang to-gether, and then they twirled around and danced. Kip in his crepe-soled shoes—he always wore crepe-soled shoes—was not a very good dancer either, but he was awkward in such a charming, boyish way. He joined the girl in a few more bars of their song, and then he was alone, singing *Play Like You Love Me* straight to Jean. The bottle of shampoo turned handsprings and the announcer, amused at the antics of the shampoo, urged everyone to buy a bottle and explained that im-partial scientific tests had proved conclusively that this shampoo left ninety-seven and one half percent less dull soap film on the hair than nine other brands on the market. The program was over for another week.

Almost immediately the telephone rang. Jean, cer-tain that it was Elaine who was calling, went into the kitchen to answer.

"Jean? Did you watch?" Elaine sounded as if she were suppressing some strong emotion.

"Yes," answered Jean breathlessly. "Wasn't he *wonderful?*"

"I practically died just watching him," said Elaine and then, speaking pointedly for the benefit of her father, added, "Of course Dad had to rattle his paper and make a lot of rude remarks, but I guess some people just don't appreciate the finer things in life."

Knowing how Mr. Mundy would react to this remark, Jean laughed. "I know," she said sympathetically. "Dad is the same way, but I just rise above it."

"Can you come over for a while?" asked Elaine.

"Sure," answered Jean. "See you in a minute." After Jean had taken her coat from the closet in the room she shared with her sister, she informed her family where she was going and added, "No homework for two weeks!"

"Aren't you going to change your skirt?" Sue, who was so skillful with needle and thread, was disturbed by the unmatched plaid. "The jog in the stripes makes your skirt look as if one half is two inches higher than the other half."

"Oh . . . I guess not," answered Jean. "We are only going to write to our pen pals. Anyway, I have to wear the skirt sometime, and I certainly don't want to wear it to school." She picked up a box of note paper that had been lying on the bookcase and looked inside to make sure she had three envelopes, because she had three letters to write: one to Japan, one to England, and a third, in shaky French, to France. Jean and Elaine always spoke of their pen pals as if the phrase was enclosed in invisible quotation marks. Pen pals were for nine- and ten-year-olds. Their correspondence was on a higher level. By writing to girls in other countries they were improving their languages and promoting better understanding between nations.

This, of course, was much more intellectual than just having fun getting mail with foreign stamps.

"Aren't you spending a lot of time at Elaine's?" asked Mrs. Jarrett, looking up from the pad of paper on her knee.

"Not much," said Jean. "I mean, what else is there to do?"

"But you saw her this afternoon after school," said Mrs. Jarrett absently, as she scribbled something on the pad of paper.

"Another contest, Mother?" asked Jean.

"Yes. Why I like Swish detergent in twenty-five words or less," answered Mrs. Jarrett. "Don't you think 'elbow-grease efficiency' would be a good phrase to use? I have heard that winning letters are always full of hyphens."

"Sounds good to me," answered Jean, her hand on the knob of the front door.

"Of course I don't like to give the impression that using Swish is work," remarked Mrs. Jarrett critically. "I don't think the judges would like that."

"You could say, 'I like Swish detergent because it makes washday such a whale of a lot of fun,'" suggested Mr. Jarrett from behind his newspaper.

"Oh, I think that is going a little too far," said Mrs. Jarrett seriously.

"Dad is just joking." Jean smiled and opened the door.

"Why not use something that rhymes?" suggested Sue. "Something like, 'I like Swish because when I Swish the clothes I have more time to doze.'"

"You can laugh all you want," said Mrs. Jarrett agreeably, "but just the same, it would help a lot if I could win a new refrigerator. Our old one goes on and off so often I think it must be on its last legs. And don't forget, I won the television set by liking peanut oil in twenty-five words or less."

"Better let Dandy out as long as you are going," Mr. Jarrett told Jean.

Jean snapped her fingers to the beagle, who rose reluctantly. Dandy, who had half his tail missing, had once belonged to someone on Mr. Jarrett's route. When a car door had been slammed on Dandy's tail and several inches of the tail had to be amputated, the dog could no longer be exhibited at dog shows, and his owners had no further use for him. Mr. Jarrett, who had grown fond of the dog in the course of delivering mail to the owner's house, heard that they wanted to get rid of him and offered to give him a home. When he brought Dandy home, Mrs. Jarrett protested, "But we can't afford to keep a dog." She was still protesting, usually just before payday, but the Jarretts continued to keep and to love Dandy.

"Don't stay out late," said Mr. Jarrett.

"I never do stay out late, Dad," answered Jean. Some things were just habits with parents. You would think from the way Mr. Jarrett spoke that his daughters went out with boys.

The day had been smoggy, as December days so often were, but a late afternoon breeze had swept away the ugly haze and left the night clear and sharp. The change in the weather was exhilarating to Jean. As she ran down the sidewalk, the street light behind her making her shadow dance ahead of her, she wished for something more exciting than an evening writing to pen pals.

"Come in," called out Mr. Mundy, when Jean had run up the steps and tapped on the front door.

As Jean stepped out of the cold air into the warm room, fragrant with Christmas greens, vapor formed on her glasses as quickly as if a white curtain had been jerked down before her eyes. She pulled off her glasses and waved them around to let the moisture evaporate.

"Hello there, Half Pint," said Mr. Mundy jovially.

"Mr. Mundy, I'll have you know that I am five feet one and one quarter inches tall," said Jean, who was used to being teased about her size by her best friend's father. "I was measured in gym last week."

"Imagine that," remarked Mr. Mundy. "Pretty soon you'll have to pay full price at the movies."

"Oh, Dad, cut it out," called Elaine from the kitchen. "Jean has paid full admission for years."

"I need Jean's help," said Mrs. Mundy, also from the kitchen. "Come on, Jean."

Cedar boughs were heaped on newspapers on the kitchen floor. On the table lay a stack of Christmas wreaths and a pile of wire coat hangers that had been bent into circles. Mrs. Mundy, a plump, pleasant-looking woman, was wiring greens to the circles while Elaine fastened clusters of gilded eucalyptus buds to the wreaths. Elaine, who took after her father, was tall, thin, slightly round-shouldered, and the kind of girl who could never keep her shirttail tucked in. She said Jean made her feel gawky, all knees and elbows. Jean said Elaine made her feel like someone who should buy her clothes in the children's department. "The long and the short of it," Mr. Mundy often remarked when he saw the girls together, and that was almost every day.

"What would you like me to do?" asked Jean, pleased that they were going to make wreaths instead of writing letters.

"Take the garden clippers and snip off pieces of cedar for me—limber pieces that I can bend around the wire," directed Mrs. Mundy. "When we finish another half dozen I can deliver them to the clubhouse. Our lodge is having a bridge luncheon tomorrow, and I am in charge of decorations."

"And you know Mom," said Elaine. "Always leaving everything to the last minute."

"Oh, not always," protested Mrs. Mundy, smiling.

The three worked swiftly. Jean enjoyed the fragrance of the cedar. Decorating for a party, even someone else's party, made her feel so festive she was almost
sorry to see the last coat hanger camouflaged with
green and the last cluster of eucalpytus buds wired
into place.

"There," said Mrs. Mundy, with an air of having
accomplished something. "Wouldn't you girls like to
drive over to the clubhouse with me while I deliver
these?"

The girls agreed that a ride across town would be a
pleasant change. They put on their coats and carried
the wreaths out to the car. Jean found it agreeable to
have the illusion of going someplace, of doing something different, even though she was only going along
on someone else's errand. Riding in a wreath-filled car
on the first night of Christmas vacation seemed a
promise of fun and festivity.

"Three and a half months," whispered Elaine, who
could be referring to only one thing—Kip Laddish's
personal appearance.

"Three and a half months," answered Jean fervently, as she enjoyed the lighted Christmas trees in
the windows along the street.

When they reached the clubhouse they saw light
streaming from the windows and heard bursts of music
as the door opened and closed. "Come on, girls," said
Mrs. Mundy briskly. "There's an armload for each of
us. We'll just leave them in the kitchen for tonight. I
am coming over in the morning with the rest of the
committee after the decorations from the dance have
been cleared out." The girls, with their loads of
wreaths, followed Mrs. Mundy into the building and
past the ceiling-high Christmas tree in the lobby into
the kitchen, which smelled of stale coffee. They piled
their wreaths on the long drainboard beside a row of
gallon coffeepots.

"There, that's done," said Mrs. Mundy. "Now I have a few things to attend to in the office. Why don't you girls go in and watch the dance for a few minutes?"

"Yes, let's," said Elaine eagerly, and Jean agreed. It would be fun to see what others were doing for a good time on the first night of Christmas vacation.

The girls slipped through the door into the room where the party was being held. "There are some chairs along the wall," whispered Elaine. "Let's sit there."

The two girls pulled off their coats and sat on the hard folding chairs. "I hope we don't look like wallflowers," murmured Elaine.

"Not in these school clothes. They'll know we aren't part of the crowd," answered Jean. "For us, I guess you could call dancing a spectator sport."

"I see some juniors and seniors from school," observed Elaine, "and a few fellows and girls home from college."

Jean did not answer. She was too absorbed in the scene before her. It seemed to her an enchanting picture in motion. The room was fragrant with garlands of Christmas greens, and from the center of the ceiling hung a revolving ball made of bits of mirror that cast flakes of light, like confetti, over the boys in their dark suits and the girls in their light dresses. Never had Jean seen so many pretty dresses before—dresses of net and taffeta and lace, all of them fresh and graceful. And the flowers—the girls wore flowers on their shoulders or in their hair or pinned to their sashes. The fragrance of gardenias mingled with the scent of the greens.

"Some of them are even wearing orchids," whispered Elaine.

"I know." Jean's eyes slid from the flowers to the shoes—slippers and sandals of silver and gold and

tinted satin. And for every pair of delicate shoes there
was a pair of polished black shoes.

"When I have a formal I want a pair of shoes dyed
to match," whispered Elaine. "You can buy the shoes
at Belmonts' for six ninety-nine, and the store tints
them free."

Jean felt a twinge of annoyance. She wanted to take
in the scene before her without thinking of the cost of
shoes or the problems of matching dye to swatches of
material.

"Kip Laddish has a new record of that piece the
band is playing," said Elaine. "I'm going to buy it
when I get my allowance."

The music stopped, and couples drifted to the edge
of the room. The flowers, the smiling faces, the dresses
dappled by the mirrored light made, it seemed to Jean,
one of the loveliest scenes she had ever watched.

And then quite unexpectedly a boy was standing in
front of Jean. A tall boy in a dark suit. A boy with a
pleasant smile. "May I have this dance?" he asked.

He must be speaking to someone else. Jean felt
Elaine nudge her.

"May I have this dance?" he repeated.

"Me?" Jean stared at the boy in disbelief, even
though he was standing directly in front of her. A
boy—asking Jean Jarrett to step into the scene before
her?

"Yes, you," answered the boy, with an engaging
smile.

Like a girl walking in her sleep, Jean rose from her
chair and stepped forward. The music started. The
boy put his arm around her and took her right hand
in his left. She laid her left hand on his right shoulder.
She was in the boy's arms, a part of the scene she had
been watching. She felt as if she had stepped into a
dream.

It was then that reality intruded. Jean remembered that she did not know how to dance.

The boy took a step, and Jean stumbled. "I—I'm sorry," she managed to say. "I'm not a very good dancer."

"That's all right," he said cheerfully. "I won't try anything fancy."

But he knows, thought Jean. Two steps, and already he knew she did not know how to dance. Her mind was awhirl. All she could think clearly was, My skirt. My awful homemade skirt with the jogs in the plaid. And she was wearing bobby socks and saddle shoes. Heavy, flat shoes. Sensible shoes that would wear a long time. Her hands grew icy, and her right hand, she now discovered, was sticky from the pitch on the Christmas wreaths. She stumbled. She stumbled again. She wanted to break away from this boy and flee through the crowd, but she did not have the courage. She did not understand how she had managed to get herself into this situation—it had seemed so natural and so wonderful that first moment when she had risen from her chair and stepped toward him—and now . . . this. . . .

The boy simplified his steps until he was walking to music and Jean only had to slide her feet backwards. Then she found she did not know what to do with her face. In her flat shoes she could not see over his shoulder. She was afraid of smearing lipstick on his coat so she thrust her chin upward. She found this awkward and felt that she must be wearing the strained look Dandy wore when he swam and tried to keep his chin out of water. She tried turning her face to the right. Although still not very comfortable, this was better. At least she had a good view of the shirt front of this boy, whoever he was.

They danced, or rather walked, in silence. Jean

wondered desperately how much longer the music
would go on. At the same time she was aware that the
boy smelled pleasantly of clean wool and soap. Why, I
never knew before that a boy could smell good, she
thought in surprise. She had not, in fact, thought
much about real boys at all. What boy would be interested in a fifteen-year-old girl who could pass for thir-
teen and who wore glasses, besides? Boys were people
who lived in the same neighborhood and went to the
same school. Some of them were agreeable to talk to
once in a while and some were noisy nuisances. Certainly she had not thought of any of them as dancing
partners—that would come in that vague and happy
time, the future. It had been so much easier to dream
about a boy who followed a tap-dancing bottle of
shampoo onto the television screen. With that boy she
would be dancing lightly, gracefully . . . but with
this boy, this real, live boy. . . . Well, it was all so
different from her dreams.

Jean stepped squarely on the boy's toe. "Excuse
me," she managed to say.

"That's all right," he answered.

The music stopped, and Jean felt as if she had been
set free. Then she remembered this was only a pause,
that each dance was divided into three parts. Feeling
that it was only fair to offer the boy his freedom, she
looked up uncertainly at him while she surreptitiously
wiped the palms of her clammy hands on her skirt.

The boy grinned. "You're catching on," he said.

It was nice of him to say it. Jean did not know what
to answer. She looked down at the floor and saw that
her white saddle shoes were now marked with black
polish. The boy's shoes were streaked with her white
shoe cleaner.

The music began again, the boy put his arm around
Jean, and once more she found herself propelled

around the room. She caught a glimpse of Elaine staring at her and, beside her, Mrs. Mundy watching with
amusement. How ridiculous I must look, thought
Jean, seeing herself in relation to the rest of the crowd
for the first time, walking around backward in saddle
shoes and an old blouse and that skirt—that awful
skirt—when all the other girls looked so pretty.

This time the boy stepped on Jean's toe. "I'm
sorry," he said pleasantly.

At least he was game. Jean was too miserable to answer.

The music stopped. Two down and one to go,
thought Jean, unless she could escape. The thing to do
was look this boy, whoever he was, in the eye and excuse herself quickly before the music started again.
But when she forced herself to look him in the eye, her
resolution wavered. He was so good-looking—tall with
dark hair and a jaunty bow tie. Now she knew that
she had seen him around school during the past semester. He was a senior, she was sure, but who was he?

"Do you go to Northgate High?" asked the boy.

Jean nodded. He had not remembered seeing her
around school—but why should he? And then her courage returned. "Please excuse me," she said swiftly, her
cheeks hot. "I really don't know how to dance and I
should not have accepted." She turned and as she
turned, she thought—she couldn't be sure—that he
put out his hand to stop her. She did not wait to find
out. She made her way past the other couples, the net
and taffeta of the other girls' skirts brushing against
her bare legs.

When she reached her chair against the wall, Jean
snatched up her coat. "Come on, Elaine," she whispered. "Let's get out of here!"

Elain followed her into the lobby. "Jean," she said
eagerly, "how did you have the *courage?*"

"I don't know," answered Jean weakly. "I just did. Only it wasn't courage exactly. I guess I didn't know any better."

Mrs. Mundy joined the girls beside the Christmas tree. "Jean, you did splendidly," she said warmly.

Jean managed to smile. She knew this was not true, but it was Mrs. Mundy's nature always to look at the cheerful side.

"What was his name?" asked Elaine.

"I don't know," admitted Jean.

"You don't know?" Elaine was disbelieving. "Didn't you ask him?"

"I couldn't," said Jean. I was too busy thinking about my feet." Those two feet in bobby socks and saddle shoes. "I couldn't talk and think about my feet at the same time. I—I can't even remember what he looked like. Not very clearly anyway, except that he was wearing a bow tie."

"I can," said Elaine. "He was terribly good-looking. He even had curly hair."

"Then why did he want to dance with me?" Jean was genuinely bewildered. Why should a boy want to dance with a strange girl who was not even dressed for the party?

"I don't know," said Elaine. "But he did. That's what counts."

The two girls followed Elaine's mother out to the car. "Jean," whispered Elaine, as they climbed into the back seat, "was it fun, dancing with a good-looking boy?"

"Well . . . no," said Jean honestly. "It was really pretty awful. You know—me in saddle shoes with my hands all clammy and not knowing how to dance."

"I know." There was real regret in Elaine's voice.

Mrs. Mundy pushed the starter button. "Jean, you must be very happy to have had such a nice-looking boy ask you to dance," she remarked.

"Yes," answered Jean, because Mrs. Mundy, a firm believer in positive thinking, would expect an affirmative answer. And yet she really was happy. That was the funny part of it. She had been miserable, but there was more to her feelings than that. She sensed that Elaine was holding back a flood of questions, because there were some things girls did not like to talk about in front of their mothers.

Jean was glad to have a chance to think about her experience, to try to decide how she really did feel about it. It was surprisingly difficult to remember. She was left with an impression of a boy's pleasant voice, of his dark woolen shoulder and white shirt-front, of music and the feel of his toe treading on hers, of other couples moving past and of her own confusion.

All at once it became important that Jean remember everything, every single little detail. She tried to recall what music had been played, but she could not. The only thing she could recall distinctly was the clear wool-and-soap smell of the boy. The rest was just a blur.

It was all so puzzling. Jean had had an embarrassing, uncomfortable experience, and yet it had left her feeling happy. Never before had she felt happy over her own embarrassment. And then she understood. For the first time in her life a boy had singled her out of a crowd. A boy, a real live boy. . . . Why, the future had arrived!

Mrs. Mundy stopped the car in front of the Jarretts' house and, after saying good night, waited until Jean was safely in the house.

The living room was empty. Jean snapped off the light and went to the room she shared with her sister. Sue was sitting in front of the portable sewing machine set up on the table which the girls shared for study and for sewing. On the bed was a row of red and green felt slippers with turned-up toes. On the toe of each was a little bell.

"How perfectly darling!" exclaimed Jean.

"This represents most of my Christmas shopping. I can make them for practically nothing, and they would cost a lot to buy," answered Sue. "I love to make things out of felt. It never has to be hemmed."

Without removing her coat, Jean sat down on the bed and absently picked up a slipper and swung it back and forth to make the bell jingle.

"You look sort of dazed," remarked Sue.

Jean dropped the slipper and looked at her sister. "I guess I am."

"Why?" asked Sue amiably. "Too many Kip Laddish records at Elaine's house?"

"You know, it was the funniest thing," said Jean, "but something nice really did happen."

CHAPTER
2

The first thing Jean discovered after the dance was that once a boy singles a girl out of a crowd for the first time, her life is never quite the same again. She discovered this when she started to clean her saddle shoes. She shook the bottle of cleaner, poured a little of the fluid onto a cloth, picked up her shoe, and looked thoughtfully at the streaks of black shoe polish on the white leather. Smiling to herself, she put the cap back on the bottle of cleaner and returned the bottle to the closet. There was no hurry about rubbing off the marks the boy's shoes had made on hers. Instead of cleaning her shoes as she always did on Saturday morning, she sat staring dreamily at her smudged toes, while in her mind's eye she saw the boy, giving his shoes a last-minute shine. Perhaps he had been whistling as he bent over and snapped a cloth back and forth across his toes. Then he must have straightened up, put away the polish, slipped into his coat, and paused, still whistling, in front of his mirror to straighten his tie and run a comb through the hair Elaine had said was curly.

Jean enjoyed the scene so much she ran through it once more, this time adding wall-to-wall carpeting to the boy's room and having him tuck a folded handkerchief into his breast pocket. And what about his shoes this morning? Was he polishing off the white marks she had left on the black leather? Maybe that was what he was doing this very minute. It was the beginning of a period of absentmindedness for Jean.

And then there was the matter of clothes. Jean hung the mismatched plaid skirt in the back of her closet and hoped her mother would not notice that she did not wear it. She longed for a closet full of pretty clothes. Until now she had been satisfied with the dresses her mother made for her or that she made for herself, and with the sweaters that her mother bought at sales. Now Jean looked at fashions in the morning paper and lingered over the advertisements of the Northgate Apparel shop. She spent a lot of time in the bathroom, where the light was best, looking at the back of her shoulder-length hair in a hand mirror, pulling a comb through her locks, and shaking her head to make her hair swing back and forth like a model in a television commercial for shampoo. Her family often had to pound on the bathroom door and remind her that the bathroom was not hers exclusively.

If the change that five minutes with a boy brought about in Jean was strange, the change that the same five minutes brought about in Elaine was even stranger. While Jean was content to daydream about the real live boy, Elaine prepared to organize. Jean discovered this the Saturday evening after the girls had carried the wreaths into the clubhouse.

Because Mr. Mundy was part owner of a plumbing business and for the sake of his business belonged to a number of clubs and service organizations, the Mundys led an active social life. They often went out on Saturday evening and, rather than leave Elaine at home alone, they usually invited Jean to keep her company. These evenings had fallen into a pattern that both girls enjoyed. Jean arrived late in the afternoon, sometimes with her pajamas and toothbrush, if the Mundys expected to be out late. Mrs. Mundy gave them some money to buy the ingredients of their own dinner. The two girls walked to the nearby shopping center to plan their menu and to market, studying prices and trying to buy as many of their favorite foods as possible. There were three rules in their private game: except for seasonings they must not use anything in the Mundys' cupboards or refrigerator for their meal, they could not add any money of their own to the sum Mrs. Mundy had given them, and they must spend every penny of this sum. To accomplish this required careful figuring on little slips of paper. On this Saturday they returned to Elaine's house with two pork chops, one large avocado which was a great bargain because it was bruised, two artichokes, a papaya which they selected because neither of them had ever tasted this fruit, and, to use up the last pennies, three Greek olives from the delicatessen. The third olive they would meticulously cut in two.

"You lucky girls!" exclaimed plump Mrs. Mundy, when she saw the groceries. "The calories you can consume and not gain an ounce." She tugged at her skirt as if she felt it might be too tight, kissed both girls lightly on the cheek, and said, "Have a good time and don't forget to go to bed. We should be home by midnight."

"We don't want to see the bedroom light go off as we drive up the driveway," said Mr. Mundy. "And don't forget to wash the dishes."

"We always wash them, Dad," said Elaine, "unless we burn something and have to soak the pan."

"Jean, do you mind if I tell you something?" Elaine asked, when her parents had left and the girls had set about preparing their meal. She continued, regardless of whether Jean minded or not. "You should wear your bangs shorter."

"My bangs?" repeated Jean, putting her hand to her forehead.

"Yes," said Elaine. "Sometimes you let them get too long and then you go around sort of peering out from under them."

"I do?" Dismayed by this picture of herself, Jean brushed her bangs away from her forehead.

"Yes. You are the gamin type and you should wear them short," said Elaine, unwrapping the pork chops.

Jean laughed, amused at hearing Elaine speak in fashion-magazine language. "I thought a gamin was a ragged little boy."

"You know what I mean," said Elaine impatiently. "Sort of little and . . . well, you know. And another thing—do you have to wear your glasses all the time?"

"I'm pretty nearsighted," said Jean. "Anyway, I don't mind them too much anymore. They have become a part of me."

"But the point is, you could get along without them in the halls at school without actually walking into the wall," Elaine said. "And you want to look your best the next time you see the boy. You're lucky you don't squint, the way some people do when they take off their glasses."

Jean giggled. "Without my glasses I'm not sure I could tell him from the principal."

"Don't be silly. Of course you could." Elaine was very positive. "For one thing the principal is about six inches shorter."

Jean cut the stems from the two artichokes. "Oh, Elaine, what difference does it make? He won't even remember me."

"Of course he will remember you," said Elaine. "He danced with you, didn't he?"

"I wouldn't exactly call it dancing," said Jean, "but he did have a good view of the top of my head. And you know something? I still can't remember what he looked like. I mean—it all happened so fast and I was so surprised I felt confused."

"I remember," said Elaine.

Jean laid down the paring knife and the artichoke she was trimming. "Elaine, what difference does it make? The whole thing was a horrible mistake. He will never look at me again, even if he does remember me—and I almost hope he doesn't. He probably just asked me to dance because he felt sorry for me or something."

"He didn't feel sorry for *me*," Elaine pointed out. "Anyway, I don't think boys ask girls to dance because they feel sorry for them."

Jean was silent. She was turning over in her mind, as she had so many times since the incident, the possible reasons why the perfectly strange boy had asked her to dance. And why he had chosen her instead of Elaine. It might have been better if he had asked Elaine, who at least knew how to dance, because she had joined the junior high school dancing class when she was in the seventh grade. Jean had not been able to, because at the time the Jarretts could not spare the nine dollars that the class cost. But perhaps Elaine was right about the glasses. Maybe she could get along without them between classes. If one boy had noticed her, perhaps another boy might come along. . . .

Elaine gave Jean little time for daydreaming. "Now the first thing you have to do," she said, as she stood with a fork poised over the sizzling pork chops, "is to learn to dance. After dinner we can play some records and I'll show you what I have learned. We can practice all during Christmas vacation. After all, if the boy asked you once, he might ask you again and"—Elaine paused significantly—"he might have a friend."

So that was why Elaine was taking such an interest in Jean's future. Jean carefully slipped the skin from the avocado, leaving the fruit as smooth as green velvet. "I guess it wouldn't hurt to practice," she said. "Not that anything will ever come of it."

And so Jean practiced dancing under Elaine's direction during the rest of Christmas vacation. Step, step, slide, slide, step, step. "This is the basic step," Elaine explained, "but it is more fun with a boy." Step, step, slide, slide, step, step. When Mr. Mundy saw what the girls were doing, he took an interest and insisted on dancing them around the living room a few times. The girls were polite about this, but they did not feel he was much help. His dancing was so old-fashioned.

Jean began to half wish that when school started the boy would recognize her, seek her out, and say something to let her know he had not minded those few minutes spent with her. She wouldn't even expect him to ask her for a date. She would just like to know that a good-looking boy felt friendly toward her and would pay her a little attention beyond saying, "Hi," in the halls. That was the trouble with her and Elaine and a lot of other girls—nobody paid any attention to them. Jean and Elaine had both had a left-out feeling since they had transferred from junior to senior high school.

Northgate High School, the only high school in the city, seemed so big, so full of strange faces, that they felt lost in the crowds that swarmed the corridors.

One evening when the practice session ended, Elaine sat down with her long legs over the arm of a chair, helped herself to a handful of peanuts, and began to eat them one at a time. "Wouldn't it be wonderful if we got to be popular?" she asked. "Dates, committees, getting elected to offices, more dates. . . ."

"It's funny," said Jean thoughtfully, "but I don't think I even want to be popular."

"Every girl wants to be popular." Elaine was positive about this.

"I don't." This time Jean was positive too. "I'm too—too quiet. I wouldn't want to call a meeting to order or even read the minutes. And I would be miserable if I had to be a rally girl. Not that there is any danger of that."

"Not me," said Elaine. "I would simply adore swishing a couple of pompons around in front of the whole student body." She added, with a note of regret, "Except that I am taller than all the yell leaders."

"I would rather be part of the crowd cheering for the team," said Jean, nibbling a peanut.

"And when the school puts on the variety show I would like to be right out in the middle of the stage, with everybody applauding madly," said Elaine, "although I don't know exactly what they would applaud me for. I can't do anything special."

Jean giggled. "You could do that *Captain Jinks of the Horse Marines* tap dance we learned in gym. The one where we had to paw the ground with our feet."

Elaine leaned back against the arm of her chair and laughed. "I want people to applaud, not die laughing," she said. Then she sighed gustily. "I guess I don't have a thing to worry about. Nobody is going to ask me to swish a pompon in front of the rooting section or ask me to dance *Captain Jinks of the Horse Marines* in the variety show."

"I would like to be more . . . a part of things at school. And to have a boy like me," said Jean, reaching for another peanut.

"The trouble with us is that we are the salt-of-the-earth type," said Elaine gloomily. "The type that gets married someday and makes some man a good wife."

Jean laughed at her friend's gloom. "I don't think that is such a terrible fate."

"Well, you know," said Elaine vaguely. "Dishpans, mops . . ."

"Diapers, budgets," added Jean, thinking that all these things were part of the life she wanted for herself. That was one reason why she was struggling to learn to sew. Still, she understood what Elaine meant. They were girls whom no one would ever expect to dance a ballet, fly an airplane, run for Congress.

"The only thing wrong with us," said Elaine, summing up the situation, "is that we are a couple of late bloomers."

And so, on the day school started after Christmas vacation, Jean, with her bangs cut short and without her glasses, got off the bus with Elaine, walked up the blurry steps, and entered a fuzzy school building.

"Come on, let's go upstairs," whispered Elaine. "If he's a senior, his locker is up there, and if we walk along sort of casually we might see him."

Jean hung back. "Oh, Elaine," she protested, without much conviction. "If I did see him I think I would *die*."

"No, you wouldn't," said Elaine, taking Jean by the arm. "Come on. We don't have much time."

Jean allowed herself to be led up the steps to the crowded corridor on the second floor. "Now act as if we were really going someplace," directed Elaine, "and pretend you aren't looking for anyone."

Jean laughed nervously. "I don't have to pretend. I can't see very far."

Timidly the two girls patrolled the length of the corridor.

"Come on, let's go back," said Elaine, when they had reached the end. "He must be up here someplace."

Jean knew it was useless to protest in the face of Elaine's determination. And she did not really want to protest, because she wanted to see that boy again. Halfway down the length of the hall, not far from the trophy case, Elaine suddenly clutched her arm. "There he is!" she whispered.

Jean's nearsighted eyes swept the faces around her. "Where?" she asked.

"Pretend you aren't looking," advised Elaine.

"I'm not," said Jean. "I can't."

"Over there against the lockers," whispered Elaine. "In the green plaid shirt."

The plaid shirt emerged from the blur and above it a face, a good-looking face which Jean had seen before and which she now felt too timid to look at for more than an instant. Blushing, she quickly looked away.

Elaine, still clutching Jean's arm, giggled nervously, and the two girls hurried to the stairs, where they ran down the steps to the first floor.

Jean put on her glasses and found it a relief to be once more in a world with clear-cut edges. "Do you think he saw me?" she asked anxiously.

"I don't know. I think so," said Elaine, with her nervous giggle. Then she sighed. "He's *so* good-looking in that plaid shirt."

"I don't care," said Jean. "I'm going to pretend I never saw him before in my life. If he did see me and remember me, he didn't bother to speak. I am just going to forget the whole thing."

Jean did not forget, however, and she found that with careful timing she could make her path cross that of the boy several times a day. Each time she snatched off her glasses just before they met, looked straight ahead, and wished she could control the blush that rushed to her cheeks. She wished . . . she wished a lot of things. She wished that she were the kind of girl people noticed, that she had lots of pretty clothes, that she were three inches taller, two years older, and did not wear glasses.

Elaine did not forget either, and the two girls became tireless collectors of information about the boy. Every afternoon, as they rode home from school on the bus or, if it was not raining, walked so Jean could save her carfare, they compared notes and added to what they had jokingly begun to call his dossier, as if they were characters in a spy movie.

Working together to compile the boy's dossier gave Jean and Elaine the cozy feeling of sharing a delightful secret. Jean had not felt as close as this to Elaine since they were in the fourth grade and had formed the exclusive TEAJ Club. The letters stood for "The Elaine and Jean" Club, and it was so exclusive that they were the only members. They had printed the initials on badges, which they had worn to school. They enjoyed the attention the badges had attracted from the rest of the fourth grade, but when the attention diminished because their classmates began to suspect that the club had no other members, the club was abandoned.

Jean filed away in her mind every scrap of information that she and Elaine gathered. She learned that the boy had five different plaid woolen shirts—the kind that had to be dry-cleaned. He usually bought the Dagwood Special instead of the regular cafeteria lunch, except on the days when he went across the street with a crowd of boys and ate a hamburger at the Shack.

Elaine, who was bolder than Jean, usually had more

information to add to the dossier. He took chemistry—
she had seen him coming out of the lab. His name was
Johnny Chessler—he had left his notebook on a table
in the library, and she had peeked inside. ("Elaine,
what if he had *seen* you?") He knew lots of girls—
wouldn't you just know—and he spent a lot of time
talking to them in the halls. He lived at 11 Madrone
Lane, high enough in the hills so that his house had a
view. His telephone number was Toyon 1-4343—she
had looked it up in the telephone book. He had a
close friend named Homer Darvey, who was much too
short for Elaine (wasn't that just her luck?) and was
sort of funny-looking, with glasses and crinkly hair,
which he wore cut short. She had seen Johnny coming
out of a sporting-goods shop with a pair of skis over
his shoulder (probably he had rented them for the
weekend) and he had driven off in a light-blue Chrysler
with a white top and license number ENK729. She
was sure of the number because she had written it
down.

Strangely, once the girls knew Johnny's name, they
rarely mentioned it. Johnny was simply "he." This was
due partly to caution (they did not want any of the
girls at school to know about their interest in
Johnny), and partly to their childish pleasure in sharing a secret. Even at home Jean referred to Johnny,
when she felt she had to talk about him, as "that boy
who danced with me that time."

The girls discovered that by riding the bus to the
end of the line and climbing four blocks up the hill,
they could walk back past Johnny's house, and this
they did. Trying to act as if they were not even looking at the house, they observed it carefully. It was a
modern house with a flat roof, and a carport instead
of a garage. Because it was built on a steep lot, there
was no front lawn but, in its place, a bank covered
with low-growing shrubs. Although there was nothing

the least bit funny about the house (it was, in fact, a house that both girls admired), Jean and Elaine always burst into a fit of giggles when they were safely past it. One Saturday they even made the walking of Dandy, a most surprised dog, an excuse for going past Johnny's house in hopes of catching a glimpse of Johnny. Jean hoped that if Johnny happened to see them he would realize that Dandy had once been a show dog, even though half his tail was missing now.

And with each shred of information that Jean stored away she found it more and more difficult to forget the boy. Johnny Chessler. Johnny. Jean squeezed her memory hard, and brought back the remembered scent of soap and clean wool and, with it, the memory of his toe treading on hers. It was not what a girl could call a beautiful memory, but it was a memory that Jean clung to. It was the only memory concerning a boy that she had to cling to.

From the school paper the girls learned that Johnny took part in the Saturday-morning broadcast, called "'Hi-times," that Northgate High presented over the local radio station. After that Jean, whose share of the Saturday housework was dusting and vacuuming the living room, always turned on the radio and listened, dustcloth in hand, for Johnny's voice. When she heard him speak, introducing a record or interviewing a basketball player, she compared his voice with her memory of the voice which had said, "May I have this dance?" She hung on every word.

Then, early in February, there came a few days of sudden spring weather. The sky was blue, with fluffy white clouds sailing above hills green from winter rains. During lunch period students sunned themselves on the high-school steps or strolled about, enjoying the warmth. It was the kind of day that made a girl wish she could throw away all her winter sweaters and skirts and go out and buy a whole new wardrobe of gay cotton dresses.

Jean, who had eaten her lunch, brought from home, with Elaine, who had bought her lunch, was eager to go outdoors and enjoy the false spring day. The two girls walked aimlessly around the school grounds, enjoying the sunshine and pausing to look at the flowering quince blooming under the windows on the side of the building that got the afternoon sun. The pink blossoms on the bare branches meant that a more lasting spring was not far away. Jean wanted to say to the other trees and shrubs, which were leafless, "Hurry up and bloom!"

It was out at the playing field that the two girls saw Johnny Chessler, with a group of boys who were clowning in the sunshine. They were taking turns seeing how far they could walk on their hands. Confident that Johnny was too busy to notice them, the girls stopped to watch. This time Johnny was wearing his blue plaid shirt, with the sleeves rolled up, and he looked, as always, extremely attractive. Gracefully he bent over, dropped his weight onto his hands, and flipped his feet into the air, spilling change out of his pocket upon the grass. He walked easily ten or twelve feet before he stood up, grinned, and accepted his change from his friend Homer, who had picked it up for him.

The breeze ruffled Jean's bangs. Johnny was *so* attractive. "I wonder how old he is," she remarked wistfully, pushing up the sleeves of her sweater.

"I know how to find out," said Elaine.

"How?" asked Jean.

"Ask him," answered Elaine.

This idea was so farfetched that Jean did not bother to comment.

"And I'm going to," announced Elaine impulsively.

Jean was aghast. "Elaine! You wouldn't!"

"Yes, I would," said Elaine, the light of daring in her eyes.

"Elaine!" protested Jean, seeing that her friend meant what she said. "No!"

Her protest was not heeded. Elaine, her head held high, marched across the playing field and through the crowd of boys, who were now playing leapfrog. Jean watched in fascination and consternation until Elaine approached Johnny. Then, because she could not bear to watch any longer, she turned her back and began to walk toward the main building, hoping that if Johnny glanced in her direction he would not think she and Elaine were together. She wanted no part of this latest inspiration of Elaine's. Sometimes you'd think it was Elaine with whom Johnny had danced.

Jean climbed the steps and entered the building, its nearly empty corridors seeming like dark tunnels after the bright spring sunlight. She walked to her locker and had just finished twirling the combination on the lock when she heard Elaine's hurried footsteps.

"Jean!" gasped Elaine, her face crimson from hurrying and from excitement. "I did it!" She leaned back against the row of lockers and clasped her notebook to her chest. "Just wait till I tell you!"

"Elaine, you didn't tell him I wanted to know, did you?" demanded Jean.

"Oh, no. Nothing like that," said Elaine, taking a big breath. Apparently she had a lot to tell. Either that, or she was enjoying making a big anecdote out of a small experience. "Well, I walked across the playing field and through this bunch of boys clowning around, and I walked up to him—he was standing by the backstop—and I stood right in front of him. He was talking to some fellows and he didn't notice me. Well, there I was, and I had to do something with all the other fellows looking at me, so I reached out and poked his arm with my finger as if I were ringing a doorbell or something—his sleeve was rolled up and his arm was brown and sort of hairy, *you* know—and all the fellows stopped talking and looked at me. Honestly, I just about *died!* But there I was, and I had to do something, didn't I?"

"You said that before," Jean reminded her.

"And so I just came right out with it. 'How old are you?' I asked. And wait till I tell you what he said!"

Jean waited.

"He grinned sort of a lazy grin and said—these were his exact words—'I'm seventeen, but tell *her* I'm nineteen.' And I said. 'Thank you,' and got away as fast as I could." Elaine, her story at an end, was out of breath.

"Oh—" was all that Jean could say. What did Johnny mean? That he had missed none of it—the strolls through the upstairs hall to catch a glimpse of him, the giggling, whispered conferences when they had seen him? Probably he had seen Elaine write his license number and thought that Jean had asked her to spy on him. "Oh, Elaine," said Jean miserably. "Why did you have to go and do it? He probably thought I asked you to."

"But don't you see?" said Elaine. "He has noticed you!"

"I guess he couldn't help it, the way we watched him and giggled as if we had never seen a boy before," said Jean, in a flat voice. "Well, now we know we aren't invisible. We must have thought we were. Let's just forget the whole thing." It wasn't as though she had ever really known Johnny, or anything like that. To him, she was just a girl he had danced with once (but why? *why?*) and now he must think she was a very silly person. And he would be right. She *was* silly.

"I don't see why you feel that way," said Elaine. "I thought you would be pleased that he had noticed you. I would be."

"I am never going to look at him again," resolved Jean. "Well, my next class is in the annex. I guess I might as well go out before the halls are mobbed."

"If that's the way you feel," said Elaine humbly, "I am terribly sorry. I just thought. . . ."

Jean walked toward the bright square of light made by the open door at the end of the corridor. Students were beginning to straggle in from outdoors. Automatically Jean nodded and spoke to acquaintances, but her mouth and eyes refused to smile. How could she ever have behaved as she had? Why, everyone in school must know she had a crush on Johnny! And everyone must know how hopeless it was, because Johnny was a senior, attractive and popular in his collection of expensive woolen shirts. And who was she? Just a fifteen-year-old girl, small for her age, and noticed by practically no one at all.

As Jean walked through the doorway and emerged from the dark hall into the sunlight, she almost had to close her eyes because of the sudden brightness. At the foot of the steps, as she was turning toward the annex, she bumped into a boy. "Excuse me," she said, and stepped to the right. Unfortunately, the boy stepped to his left at the same moment. Then they both stepped to Jean's left and Jean was suddenly aware that she was facing a blue plaid shirt. This boy was Johnny.

"Say, what is this, a minuet?" asked Johnny, and then smiled when he recognized Jean. It was a genuine smile, warm and friendly. "Oh—hi," he said. "How's the cute girl?"

"Hi," answered Jean, and fled toward her classroom in the annex. She wondered where she had found the breath to speak that one syllable, because now she could scarcely breathe. Johnny had smiled and had actually spoken to her! He had called her a cute girl. Maybe Elaine was right after all. Maybe she ought to be pleased that Johnny had noticed her.

As she slipped into her seat, Jean's emotions were in a snarl. Johnny had remembered her, or anyway noticed her at school, and now he had smiled and spoken and called her a cute girl. Nobody had ever called her a cute girl before. Cute? What did it really mean? It was a word she had often used carelessly, like all the other girls, but she had never thought of it as a boy's word. Kittens were cute. Puppies were cute. Hats were cute.

Jean slid out of her seat and walked to the dictionary on the stand by the blackboard. She turned toward the end of the *C's* and ran her finger down the columns until she came to the word *cute*. She studied the definition intently: "cute (kut), adj., cuter, cutest. 1. *U.S. Colloq.* Pleasingly pretty or dainty." Pleasingly pretty or dainty. Then the word really was a compliment!

Jean, who had been called Midge or Half Pint so often that she had come to think of herself as insignificant, now felt herself blossoming. A boy had called her a cute girl, which meant pleasingly pretty or dainty, *and she had been wearing her glasses.* She began to feel that she really was pleasingly pretty or dainty—in the United States in a colloquial or conversational sense, of course.

Suddenly Jean laughed out loud. Colloquially in the United States was the very best way for a girl who lived in California to be pleasingly pretty or dainty.

"The dictionary is funny?" remarked the boy in the nearest seat.

"My favorite joke book." Jean smiled blithely.

"Dames," muttered the boy, and although he tapped his forehead he returned Jean's smile.

Jean felt as if the boy were noticing her for the first time. Prettily and daintily she slid into her seat.

CHAPTER
3

After the near collision on the steps, Johnny began to speak to Jean whenever he saw her at school. Every word he spoke increased her happiness—someone was noticing her at last. "Hi. How's the cute girl?" he would drawl, while she colored in the light of his smile. Sometimes he would say simply, "Hello, Jean." This made her even happier, because the words told her that Johnny had taken the trouble to learn her name. She imagined him stopping someone in the hall and asking, "Say, who is that girl over there? The cute one."

One cloudy afternoon late in February, Jean, quite by accident, made an important discovery. The last class of her day was Clothing I. Her project for this class was a dress with set-in sleeves, a problem that had given her considerable trouble. No matter how many times she basted those sleeves into the armholes, they persisted in puckering at the shoulders. That afternoon Jean had grimly ripped out her basting threads twice, and by pinning the sleeves every quarter of an inch (so that was the secret!), she finally had them basted smoothly into place.

Jean took her work to Mrs. Rankin, the sewing teacher, to have it approved, but she was put off while her teacher interrupted the class to make an announcement. The Costume Club, whose adviser was Mrs. Rankin, needed members, and anyone who studied

Clothing was eligible. Jean, who always thought of clubs as activities for other people but not for herself, paid little attention to this announcement. Sue was taking extra courses in typing and shorthand and did not have time for clubs, and so Jean, used to following in her sister's footsteps, had not thought about joining any clubs either. By waiting with her sewing in hand until Mrs. Rankin was through speaking, Jean finally had her work approved, but by that time the class was nearly over and all the sewing machines were occupied.

Jean made up her mind that she was not going to leave until she had those sleeves stitched into her dress. She was tired of sleeves, she was tired of the dress, and she wanted the whole project out of the way. She whiled away the time tidying her sewing box. This had been an exasperating afternoon.

"Are you going to join the Costume Club?" whispered Mitsuko Yamoto, who sat across the table from Jean.

"No, I don't think so," said Jean, without thinking at all.

"I am," said Mitsuko. "Everybody says it is lots of fun to be behind the scenes at the senior play and the variety show and things. The school rents most of the costumes and all the club has to do is press them, fit them, and see that the right people get into them."

"Come on, Jean, why don't you join?" asked another girl who shared the table.

Someone vacated a sewing machine—fortunately one of the good ones—and Jean, intent on her sleeves, hurried to get it before someone else did and did not bother to answer the girl's question. She stitched slowly and carefully. While she stitched in the right sleeve, the bell rang, but she went on working. She was about to stitch the left sleeve when Elaine came into the sewing room.

"Oh, there you are," said Elaine. "I've been looking all over for you. Aren't you going home?"

"Not until I finish this sleeve," answered Jean. "I have had to rip it out so many times I don't dare try to hurry with it."

"I guess I'll run along," said Elaine. "Mother wanted me to come straight home today so we could do some shopping."

Jean successfully stitched the sleeve, put away her sewing things, gathered up her books, and hurried out of the room, very nearly bumping into Johnny and his friend Homer Darvey, who were walking down the hall. "Oh—hello," she said, startled at seeing Johnny.

"Hi," answered Johnny, with a grin.

"Hi," echoed Homer.

Because the two boys were obviously leaving the building by the same door she always used, Jean found herself walking with them. In a panic she tried to think of something to say.

"Do you take sewing?" Johnny asked.

"Yes," answered Jean, longing for witty words to spring to her lips.

"I didn't think girls knew how to sew anymore," remarked Johnny.

"Oh, yes," answered Jean. "Practically everybody sews. Girls, I mean." It was silly to feel so confused, just because she was walking down the hall with a boy—two boys—but Jean could not help it.

"I was just telling Homer about my trip to the mountains last weekend," remarked Johnny, as they left the building and walked down the steps.

"Do you ski?" asked Jean, knowing very well that he did.

"Every chance I get," answered Johnny. "I drove up early Saturday morning with some fellows. One of them has a cabin."

"Then you must have run into that storm I read

about in the papers," said Jean, pleased that she could add to the conversation.

"I'll say we did," said Johnny. "It looked pretty threatening when we got there—the wind was blowing and the clouds were getting lower all the time—so we decided to get in some skiing before we took time to unload our food or our sleeping bags. Well, I was up on the mountain when the storm broke. The wind must have been blowing sixty miles an hour when I came down that mountain, and the snow was so thick it seemed to be coming from all directions at once. I didn't know whether I was going to make it back to the cabin without hitting a tree or a boulder, or not. And I wasn't sure where the other fellows were."

"Weren't you scared?" asked Jean.

"Some, but I knew that if I kept going downhill I would come to the cabin," said Johnny, his gestures suggesting skiing.

Jean could see him, slim and handsome in his ski clothes, skiing through the blizzard. "What happened? Did you make it all right?"

"It took some doing, but I finally got down that mountain," said Johnny. "I could hardly see the cabin. Well, the way the snow was drifting I thought we might get snowed in before the week end was over. Then I remembered the sleeping bags and all the food in the car, and I thought I better get it unloaded before the car got buried. So I left my skis on the porch and sort of felt my way over to the car. I had just opened the door to take out a box of groceries from the floor of the back seat, when I happened to look up and there was the biggest bear I have ever seen. He was so close I could have shaken hands with him."

"Johnny!" exclaimed Jean. "What did you do?"

"I can tell you I didn't waste any time getting into that car and slamming the door," Johnny went on. "Well, that bear went prowling around the car—I

guess he must have smelled the bacon. Bears like bacon, you know. Well, there I was shut in the car with
the bear snuffling around. Sometimes the car would
shake and I knew he was trying to break in. I was
really caught in a trap. I couldn't chase the bear away,
and I didn't dare get out." Johnny paused dramati-
cally.

Jean waited in suspense for Johnny to go on with
the story. He smiled down at his eager audience, enjoying the suspense he had created.

Then Homer spoke. "Except that bears hibernate in
the winter," he said seriously.

Jean and Johnny stared at Homer and then shouted
with laughter. His statement of fact was such an anti-
climax.

"Homer, I have never had the rug pulled out from
under me quite so fast," said Johnny, slapping Homer
on the back. "Oh, well. It was a good story while it
lasted."

Earnest, earth-bound Homer, with no imagination
at all, thought Jean. How like him to spoil a good
story. "But maybe this bear had insomnia," suggested
Jean. "Maybe he couldn't sleep, so he got up to fix
himself a snack."

"Thanks, Jean. You're my pal," said Johnny, smiling down at her as they stood on the sidewalk. "Well,
so long."

"So long," said Homer.

"Good-by," said Jean, and stood a moment watching
Johnny as he walked toward the parking lot with Homer. Johnny was everything she had hoped he would
be—interesting, full of fun, the kind of boy who
would make up for a girl's shyness. Jean chose to walk
home along a street lined with cherry trees flowering
like pink clouds in the sharp breeze. That was one
of the nice things about Northgate. In the flat part of
town the streets were lined with different kinds of

flowering trees. Jean could walk to school on a plum street and walk home on a cherry street. Jean reached out and caught a pink petal as it drifted to the ground. Johnny had walked down the hall with her!

After that Jean took to lingering in the sewing room after school, so that she could leave at the time Johnny might be coming down the hall. At first Jean made up excuses for not being able to leave when Elaine came for her, but finally, when she saw that Elaine's feelings were hurt she whispered, so none of the other girls would hear, "Look, Elaine, if I leave just a little later, sometimes I run into Johnny and he walks down the hall with me."

"So that's it! I was afraid maybe you were mad at me about something." Comprehension sparkled on Elaine's face. "Don't worry about me. I'll keep out of your way." Naturally in a situation like this a boy took precedence over a girl. "Good luck and happy hunting!"

"I'm not using a bow and arrow." Jean could not help laughing at Elaine's expression. "I knew you would understand," she said seriously, thinking that one of the reasons she valued Elaine's friendship was Elaine's cheerful acceptance of whatever she wanted to do.

Once Jean found Johnny and Homer waiting for her outside the classroom door. Actually *waiting* for her! This, Jean felt, was significant, and after that if she did not see the two boys, she waited for them to come. When Jean could find no reason for lingering any longer by the door of the sewing room, when she had reread half a dozen times the schedule of classes posted outside the door, when she had started to leave and stopped, pretending to go through her notebook looking for something she might have forgotten, she walked home alone—and missed the companionship of Elaine.

"Hasn't Johnny come yet?" one of the girls in the sewing class asked Jean one afternoon.

"Johnny?" Jean pretended surprise. "Oh, I wasn't waiting for Johnny."

Once Homer appeared alone. Jean could not avoid walking out of the building with him. "Where's Johnny?" she asked.

"Trying out for the variety show," answered Homer.

Jean remembered hearing the announcement of the tryouts in the morning bulletins for the past week. The show was to be built around the theme "Through the Years," and any student or group of students who had an act could try out. Jean, who had no desire for the spotlight, had passed over the announcement without giving it any thought. Now her thoughts fell quickly into logical sequence: Johnny, variety show, costumes, Costume Club, the club's new member as of the first thing tomorrow morning—Jean Jarrett! It was the most natural thing in the world.

"What kind of an act is he trying out with?" Jean asked.

"It isn't an act exactly," explained Homer. "They need someone to be the narrator. You know, sort of hold the acts together, and he is trying out for that part."

What sort of costume would a narrator wear? A circus ringmaster's costume? A different costume for each act? Top hat, white tie, and tails? How handsome Johnny would look in evening clothes! "Don't you want to be in the show?" Jean asked, because she felt she had to make conversation with Homer as they left the building. Boys like Homer never took part in variety shows.

"I'm already in it," said Homer. "I play a violin in the orchestra."

"That's nice," said Jean vaguely, as they reached the

foot of the steps. "Well—good-by." She did hope Johnny would wear evening clothes.

The next day Jean found Johnny and Homer waiting by the sewing-room door. Johnny told her that he had been chosen to narrate the variety show and she told him that she had been sure he would get the part and that since she was a member of the Costume Club, she would be seeing him at rehearsals. Everything, she felt, was working out very nicely indeed.

Then there was one dreadful day when Jean, who had waited too long by the sewing-room door, was about to give up and leave when she saw Johnny and Homer coming toward her with another girl, a girl named Peggy Jo. Johnny, who was smiling at Peggy Jo, was engrossed in telling her something that required broad gestures.

Jean felt a pang of pure despair. She now had a rival for her brief walk with Johnny, and that rival was Peggy Jo, who was tall, quiet, and beautiful, but a girl who wore her beauty carelessly as if it were of no interest to her. Her long fair hair was twisted into an untidy knot at the nape of her neck. She was wearing a baggy brown skirt and a tan suède jacket that needed cleaning. She looked, Jean thought, like a girl who would not bother to wash her face before going to bed. But for all her carelessness there was something about Peggy Jo that made people aware of her. What that something was Jean did not know, but she did know that she herself lacked this quality. That made it even harder to see Johnny walking with Peggy Jo.

Jean was about to slip back into the sewing room, to allow Johnny to pass without seeing her, when Johnny looked directly at her. Jean was embarrassed to have him see her waiting for him when he was with another girl. She hesitated, not knowing how to handle the situation, and while she hesitated Johnny winked at her. He looked straight into her eyes and winked. And sud-

denly everything was all right again. That wink told
her that Peggy Jo did not really matter, that he liked
Jean, and that he could not really help it, because
Peggy Jo came along and walked down the hall with
him.

Jean smiled at Johnny and walked out of the building alone. She wondered where Elaine was, and
thought how much fun she and Elaine used to have
talking over the events of their day as they walked
home from school. It almost seemed as if she and
Elaine were growing apart lately. Elaine seemed so
busy—she had even managed to get a part in the variety show. A group of girls from her gym class planned
to perform an Indian hoop dance and had asked
Elaine to join them. It was scarcely a part to bring an
applauding student body to its feet, but Elaine, a long-
legged and enthusiastic Indian, was ostentatiously
busy with rehearsals. Jean hoped that as a new member of the Costume Club she would not only see more
of Johnny but also of Elaine.

Then one Friday when Johnny and Homer had
walked out of the building with Jean, Johnny turned
to her and instead of saying good-by, said, "Are you
doing anything tomorrow night?"

"Why . . . no," admitted Jean.

"I thought I might drop around awhile if you are
going to be home," said Johnny.

"I—I would love to have you," answered Jean,
frantically trying to think what she could do with her
family when a boy came to call. "I mean—I really
would."

"I'll see you around eight," said Johnny.

"That will be nice," answered Jean, expecting him
to ask where she lived.

Johnny grinned. "So long," he said. "I'll see you tomorrow night." Apparently he already knew where she
lived.

"So long," said Homer.

Jean wasted a second's thought, as she did almost every day, in wondering what Johnny saw in an unimaginative boy like Homer. Then, elated, she hurried straight to Elaine's house. "Guess what!" she burst out, when Elaine met her at the door.

"You have a date with Johnny!" guessed Elaine.

It was blissful to be able to answer yes.

"Come in and tell me everything. Absolutely everything!" said Elaine.

"There isn't an awful lot to tell," admitted Jean and told Elaine what little there was to tell.

"Golly. He really asked you for a date. Now maybe there is hope for me." Elaine did not try to conceal her admiration. "I was going to ask you over for supper tomorrow night, but now that you are busy, I think I'll ask Maxine instead."

When Jean reached her own small house, she had no recollection of having walked there. She had been thinking about the house and how tiny it was and how awkward it would be trying to entertain Johnny, with the whole family sitting in the living room. She walked into the bedroom, where Sue was sitting at their table studying several leaflets advertising dress patterns, the sort of leaflets given away at pattern counters in department stores.

Jean could not wait to break the news. "Sue, guess what. Johnny Chessler is coming over to see me tomorrow night!"

"Johnny *Chessler*?" exclaimed Sue.

"Yes." Jean could not help feeling indignant at the way Sue spoke. "Is there anything wrong with that?"

"No. No, of course not," Sue said slowly. "Was *he* the boy who danced with you that time?"

"Yes." Jean's feelings were still slightly ruffled.

"Oh. I knew you were interested in the boy who danced with you and I knew you talked to Johnny

once in a while, but. . . . Well, it just never occurred
to me that they were the same boy," Sue explained.
"Johnny is in my English class and . . . I just never
thought about you and Johnny together, is all."

Jean looked speculatively at her sister. Sue was such
a quiet girl, it was not often easy to tell what she was
thinking. Could it be, Jean wondered, that Sue liked
Johnny herself? Poor Sue, it wasn't going to be easy to
have her younger sister dating first, especially since
Sue had already said she wanted to meet a nice boy.
Well, that was life.

Sue studied a page of dresses designed in Paris. "I
can't picture anyone I know wearing these," she remarked and then said, as if it had been Jean's date
with Johnny that she had been thinking about all the
time, "What are you going to do with him when he
gets here?"

"I don't know exactly," Jean confessed. Then she
lowered her voice and asked, "What am I going to do
about Mother and Dad? There's no place for them to
go." Tactfully she refrained from saying, "And you,
too."

"Don't worry about me," said Sue, as if she had
heard the unspoken words. "I can sew or study in our
room. But I don't know about Dad. . . ."

Once more Jean went over the house in her mind. A
living room not much larger than a nine by twelve
rug, a dining room that was practically part of the living room, two bedrooms, one bathroom, a kitchen that
was just a kitchen and not a family room like those
pictures in house and garden magazines, a breakfast
nook that showed how old the house was, because
houses were not built with breakfast nooks anymore.
That was all. It would help if the breakfast nook was
a breakfast room, but it was not. It was so awfully . . .
nooky.

"Dad may be a problem," agreed Jean, wishing that

a rumpus room or a family room or any kind of extra space would suddenly attach itself to the house.

"Maybe we could move the television set into the breakfast nook and pretend we wanted to see something during supper," suggested Sue. "If we didn't move it back. Dad might just happen to sit there and watch it."

"That won't work," said Jean, pleased that Sue was entering into her plans in spite of any feelings she might have about the date. "You know Dad won't allow television during meals."

"I guess you're right," said Sue. "But don't worry. We'll think of something."

"We'll have to," said Jean, "but I don't know what. I can't expect Mother and Daddy to go to bed at eight o'clock, just because Johnny is coming over to see me."

Sue pushed aside the fashion leaflets and smiled at her sister. "We'll manage Dad somehow," she said. "He may be strict in some ways, but underneath it all he is just an old softy."

"But you never can tell what he is going to be strict about," Jean reminded her sister. "Look how he feels about baby-sitting."

Jean waited until suppertime to break the news to her mother and father. When everyone had been served she said as matter-of-factly as she could manage, "A boy named Johnny Chessler is coming over to see me tomorrow night."

"Why, how nice, dear," said Mrs. Jarrett. "Chessler? I don't recall hearing the name. What is he like?"

"Well. . . ." Jean hesitated, wondering how to describe a boy like Johnny to her mother and father. She did not know how to explain that Johnny was handsome and charming and all the things a girl would like a boy to be. "He—he is nice-looking, with curly hair, and he wears the most beautiful woolen shirts, the

kind that have to be dry-cleaned, and he is—oh, I
don't know. . . ."

"You are telling us what he looks like," said Mr.
Jarrett, "but what I want to know is, is he good
enough for my daughter."

"Oh, Daddy," said Jean with a nervous laugh. Her
father was teasing, she knew, but she understood him
well enough to know that beneath his banter was a
serious note.

"And what I want to know," said Sue, "is how she is
going to entertain a boy. We can't all sit around the
living room and stare at him."

Jean mentally thanked her sister for bringing up
this touchy problem.

"No young whippersnapper is going to drive me out
of my house," said Mr. Jarrett.

The sisters exchanged a glance that said they understood their father was not entirely joking. "Now,
Dad," said Sue, "don't start playing the heavy father."

"We'll manage somehow," said Mrs. Jarrett reassuringly. "Of course the girls will be entertaining boys
and we will have to figure out a way for them to do
it."

"I'll stay in my room and study," volunteered Sue.
"I have to do it sometime this weekend and it might
as well be then. That will remove me from the scene."

"Your father and I will want to meet him," said
Mrs. Jarrett.

"Of course," agreed Jean. "He would think it was
peculiar if I didn't have any family around at all."

Mrs. Jarrett sighed. "I do wish we could buy a
larger house. Or at least build onto this one. Perhaps I
should enter that contest I saw announced the other
day."

"What is the prize this time?" asked Mr. Jarrett.
"Not a live kangaroo like you thought you might win
for naming that airline."

"I thought it was rather ridiculous at the time," said Mrs. Jarrett. "The winner receives his weight in gold. Or rather the equivalent in money for writing the last line of a limerick about a new kind of home permanent."

Mrs. Jarrett's family shouted with laughter. "You don't have to enter a contest," said Mr. Jarrett. "You are worth your weight in gold already."

"Have some more potatoes, Mother," urged Jean. "Just in case you win."

"Every little ounce would help," said Sue. "How about some more dressing on your coleslaw?"

"Just don't forget—I won the television set," Mrs. Jarrett reminded her family.

"But nobody has said what I am going to do with Johnny," Jean said, bringing the conversation back to the original problem.

"Just who is the fellow, anyway?" asked Jr. Jarrett.

"A boy at school." Jean resigned herself to answering questions of this sort from her father.

"If he wants to call on Jean, I am sure he is a very nice boy," said Mrs. Jarrett soothingly.

"Do you know him?" Mr. Jarrett asked Sue.

"Yes," answered Sue. "He's in my English class."

This seemed to mollify Mr. Jarrett. At least he did not ask further questions about Johnny.

"But *nobody* has said what I am going to do with him." Jean cast an anxious glance at Sue, who could be counted on to understand and help out.

"We could all have a lively game of old maid or lotto," said Mr. Jarrett.

"Daddy!" Jean could not help sounding stricken. What a dreadful idea, suggesting that Johnny play old maid or lotto with her family. He would never want to come again.

Mr. Jarrett patted Jean's hand. "Don't worry,

daughter. I was only joking. Of course you may entertain your young man." It sounded so quaint and old-
fashioned, his saying "your young man."

"The breakfast nook," said Mrs. Jarrett as Jean and
Sue rose to clear the table. "It is the only place for us.
We'll move the television set in here before Johnny
comes and after we meet him, we can come back here,
and your father can watch his television programs
while I work on a contest."

Jean and Sue exchanged a smile in the kitchen.
"Whew!" mouthed Jean silently.

"What are we having for dessert, Mother?" asked
Sue.

"Vanilla pudding," answered Mrs. Jarrett. "There is
a jar of strawberry preserves open. You might put a
dab on top of each serving to give it a little color."

"Let's call it blancmange," suggested Sue. "It sounds
so much more glamorous. When I used to read in *Little Women* about the March girls' taking blancmange
to Laurie when he was sick, I thought it must be a
great delicacy."

"Why, so did I!" exclaimed Jean. "I felt terribly dis-
illusioned to find out it was plain old vanilla corn-
starch pudding."

"I suppose this boy is going to eat us out of house
and home," commented Mr. Jarrett, as the family began to eat the vanilla pudding, or blancmange.

"That is just in the funny papers. At least I think it
is," said Jean, "but I suppose I should give him something to eat. I hadn't thought of that."

Jean thought it over. She had a vague notion that
when a boy came to see a girl, the girl usually took
him into the kitchen to raid the refrigerator. The Jarrett refrigerator, unfortunately, did not merit raiding.
Vanilla pudding and cold meat loaf were hardly the
sort of things a girl could offer a boy. And the milk.

. . . It was stored in half-gallon cartons which Mrs. Jarrett bought at the market, because she saved two and a half cents a quart, just as she bought butter in one-pound pieces because it cost five cents less than a pound of butter divided into quarters. Jean did wish they could have milk delivered in bottles from a dairy. It seemed to her that quartered butter and milk in bottles always looked so elegant in a refrigerator.

"I think you should fix something ahead of time," said Sue, who also must have been taking mental inventory of the Jarrett refrigerator. "Something you can whisk onto the table. That is what I would do if he were coming to see me."

"What table?" asked Jean. "Mother and Dad will be in the breakfast nook. Eating with a boy in the dining room is too formal."

"Serve it from a tray on the coffee table," said Sue.

"I think that is a very practical suggestion. Now don't worry, Jean. I am sure it will all work out." Mrs. Jarrett patted her daughter's hand.

Jean looked around the table at her mother, smiling at her so reassuringly, at her ruddy-complexioned father, who was so tenderhearted underneath his sternness, at Sue, who had helped her, even though it must hurt to have her younger sister have the first date. Jean was completely happy. She not only had a date with Johnny, she also had the most wonderful, understanding family in the whole world.

CHAPTER
4

Mrs. Jarrett, in galoshes and her wet-weather coat, stood by the drainboard enjoying a last-minute sip of coffee before she left for her day of selling yardage at Fabrics, Etc. "It is such miserable weather I doubt if we will be very busy today," she remarked, "even though we are having a good sale of seersucker mill ends. There are some very good buys—pieces that would make up into sturdy pajamas for children."

Sue, who was stacking the breakfast dishes, looked out the kitchen window into the gray morning. "Poor Daddy, delivering mail in this awful weather."

" 'Neither snow, nor rain, nor heat—' " began Jean, as she carried her plate from the breakfast nook into the kitchen.

" '—Nor gloom of night stays these couriers from the swift completion of their appointed rounds,' " finished Sue and her mother in unison. Mrs. Jarrett plucked a couple of dead blossoms from the brightly blooming African violet on the window sill.

"I'll have a pot of hot coffee waiting for him when he gets home this afternoon," volunteered Jean.

"That's my good girl." Mrs. Jarrett smiled at her youngest daughter. "Have you thought what you are going to serve in the way of refreshments this evening?"

Jean was happy to have the conversation turned to

the evening that lay before her. "I had thought of that dessert made of chocolate cookies with whipped cream between, because it is supposed to stand awhile before it is served, and I could make it after lunch," she said, as Sue began to wash the breakfast dishes. "Or is that too expensive?"

"I think we can manage." Mrs. Jarrett opened a cupboard, took down a canister and pulled out some of the housekeeping money, which she handed to Jean. "This should be enough. You might even buy a small jar of maraschino cherries, too."

"Thank you, Mother," said Jean. "I'll make enough so we can have some for supper, too." It did not seem right to use so much of the housekeeping money for herself and Johnny.

"And, Jean," Mrs. Jarrett continued, "be sure to plan some way to entertain him. You might get that old Chinese checker set out of the garage and set it up on the coffee table."

"Oh, Mother," protested Jean. "Nobody plays Chinese checkers anymore. That went out with bustles."

"Not quite," said Mrs. Jarrett. "Johnny doesn't have to play if he doesn't want to, but it might make things easier if you had something on hand in case you need it." Mrs. Jarrett set her empty coffee cup on the drainboard for Sue to wash. "I hope Johnny has a good time this evening. I am so glad boys are beginning to come to the house."

Jean felt that her mother's use of the plural was a little optimistic.

"What are you doing to do today, Sue?" asked Mrs. Jarrett.

"Straighten our room and then go downtown to the main library to gather material for my term paper," answered Sue. " 'Should Capital Punishment be Abolished?' "

"I didn't know high-school students were still abolishing capital punishment," remarked Mrs. Jarrett, as she opened the back door. "Well, good-by, girls. I'll try to catch the five thirty-three bus so we can have an early supper."

"Good-by, Mother," answered Jean. "I hope you sell lots of remnants."

Jean set to work cleaning the living room and dining room, and soon discovered it was much more fun to clean house for a boy than for her family. She forgot about the weather and set about trying to make the living room attractive. She ran the vacuum cleaner and used an attachment to remove Dandy's hair from the chair he slept in when no one was looking. At ten o'clock she turned on the radio to hear the Hi-times broadcast and sat, toying with the vacuum-cleaner attachment, lulled into a daydream by the smooth flow of Johnny's voice. It was too bad the program wasted time playing records—she would much rather listen to a full fifteen minutes of Johnny.

The day grew so dark that Jean had to turn on the light to dust when Hi-times was over. She had not realized the shabbiness of the furniture until now, when she tried to see her house through Johnny's eyes. She turned the cushions of the couch to find the least worn sides. She scrubbed the soiled spot on the back of her father's favorite chair with ammonia and water and then shoved the chair over a thin spot in the carpet. Her father should not object just this once, since he was going to spend most of the evening in the breakfast nook anyway. She dusted with unusual thoroughness, remembering to wipe off the window sills and the rungs of the dining-room chairs. Dustcloth in hand, she paused to look critically around the room. It was comfortable, even if it was shabby, but it needed something to brighten it, something to divert the eye—Johnny's eye—from the walls in need of a fresh coat of paint. She wished she could think of a way to hide the crack in the plaster over the door into the hall.

Jean went to the bathroom at the rear of the house and looked out into the yard in hope of seeing a few flowers that she could cut. The day was even more forbidding than she had realized. The small lawn was sodden, and the few geraniums along the fence were beaten down as if they would never have the courage to rise again. Juncos had stripped the berries from the cotoneaster in the corner of the yard, so there was no hope of creating an interesting arrangement from a few of its branches. Then Jean remembered her mother's African violet on the kitchen window sill. Its fuzzy green leaves and purple blossoms would make a spot of life and color.

Jean carried the African violet into the living room, where she tried it in front of the mirror over the mantelpiece, on the coffee table, on a lamp table, and finally back on the mantelpiece, where it stayed because, reflected in the mirror, it was almost as good as having two plants.

"Oh, Johnny, oh, Johnny, dum de de dum," Jean hummed, as she turned the plant so the most blossoms would show. Probably her mother was right about the Chinese checker set, even though Johnny might think it terribly old-fashioned of them to keep the game around. If she found conversation difficult—not that she would with a boy like Johnny, but *if* she did—she could casually make the first move, smile at Johnny, and say, "Your turn. Isn't it a quaint old game. My father simply adores it and insists we keep a set in the living room all the time." Or something like that. The more Jean thought about it, the more certain she became that this was exactly what she would have to do, except that she would have to omit the line about her father's adoring Chinese checkers. Conversation with her whole family within earshot might be difficult.

She would like to spend the evening talking to Johnny, getting to know him better. She particularly wanted to find out why he had asked her to dance that evening in December, but this sort of conversation would be impossible, unless her father happened to watch a good noisy western on television and they could talk under cover of gunfire from the breakfast nook.

Jean shoved Dandy, who appeared restless, out the back door into the storm and let him in again a few minutes later. Then as she dragged the dusty checker box out of a pile of cartons in the garage, she found another worry nagging at her. Because her father had to get up at five o'clock in the morning on work days in order to eat breakfast and be at the post office by six, he was inclined to yawn, sometimes rather noisily, by nine-thirty in the evening. Wouldn't it be dreadful if he started yawning from the breakfast nook while she and Johnny were talking? She was positive that Johnny's father, whom she pictured as a tweedy commuter with a brief case, never yawned.

When Sue had not come back from the library by lunch time, Jean prepared herself a peanut-butter sandwich, poured herself a glass of milk from a carton, and ate her chilly lunch standing beside the floor furnace with her skirt ballooned out by the hot air.

After lunch she put on her sneakers and raincoat to go to the market to buy the chocolate cookies, whipping cream, and maraschino cherries. The rain slanted against the street in sheets and she had to leap the gutters, which boiled with muddy water rushing down from the hills. She thought sympathetically of her father, his mail pouch protected by the cape on his black raincoat, who had been walking in this weather all morning. For herself she did not care. She felt exhilarated by the bad weather and even found a childish pleasure in getting her sneakers wet. What difference did it make? By evening it would all be over and when Johnny arrived the stars would be out and sparkling through the atmosphere that was now being so thoroughly washed. It almost seemed as if the whole world was being washed clean for Johnny. In the market she smiled radiantly, for no reason at all, at the boy who packed her groceries in a bag, and was surprised when he smiled back. Smiling at a boy was not so difficult after all.

Jean enjoyed puttering around the kitchen preparing dessert for Johnny. She stacked the cookies carefully with layers of whipped cream between, frosted them with graceful swirls of more whipped cream, and topped each small tower with a red cherry. She made five servings, three for her mother and father and Sue to eat for supper, and two for herself and Johnny later in the evening. She would be too excited to eat dessert with her family anyway.

When the kitchen clock told her it was almost time for her father to come home, Jean got out the percolator, measured coffee and water into it, and set it over one of the burners on the gas stove. While she waited for the coffee to perk, she leaned on the window sill of the breakfast nook and scanned the sky for even one light spot in the dark clouds. It was a soggy, soggy day and for the first time Jean began to wonder if it really would clear up before eight o'clock. The coffee began a few tentative eruptions into the glass percolator knob before it settled into a rapid perk. Come on, weather, thought Jean intently. Clear up, clear up, clear up for Johnny.

The kitchen was filled with the fragrance of hot coffee, and Jean, who timed coffee by her sense of smell rather than by the clock, turned down the heat under the percolator. Her father should be home by now. Clear up, clear up for Johnny, she went on thinking. Through the window she saw Sue, her umbrella held low against the wind, hurrying up the driveway, and hastened to open the back door for her.

"M-m-m, hot coffee!" exclaimed Sue, handing her wet umbrella to Jean, who thrust it into the sink to drip. "I'm starved. I skipped lunch, because everything cost so much downtown. Where's Daddy?"

"He hasn't come home yet," answered Jean, thinking that the cold air had made Sue's face glow until she was actually pretty. "How would you like me to make you a delicious peanut-butter sandwich, specialty of the house?"

"Would you?" asked Sue gratefully, as she glanced at the kitchen clock. "He shouldn't be this late even if the weather is awful."

"At least all the dogs that don't like mailmen will be inside on a day like this," observed Jean, spreading peanut butter with a lavish hand. "Want some coffee with your sandwich?"

"Love it." Sue removed her wet coat and hung it on a corner of the kitchen door so it would dry over the linoleum. Then she clasped both hands around the hot cup Jean handed her. "This feels good. My hands are practically numb, they are so cold."

"Get the information for your paper?" Jean cut the sandwich diagonally and laid it on a plate.

"Enough to make a good start, even though the book I need most is out," answered Sue, carrying the sandwich and coffee into the breakfast nook. "And Jean, you will never guess who I ran into in the reference room!"

"The reference librarian?" guessed Jean, joining her sister at the breakfast table with a cup of milk flavored with coffee.

"Silly," said Sue. "No. Kenneth Cory. I hadn't seen him for ages. Not since he moved out of the neighborhood."

"You mean Old Repulsive?" The words escaped

Jean's lips almost involuntarily. The expression that crossed Sue's face made her instantly regret that she had recalled the nickname the neighborhood children, with the cruelty natural to childhood, had once given this boy.

"Yes, Old Repulsive. Only he isn't anymore," said Sue. "I almost didn't know him at first. You know how he used to have buck teeth with bands on them? Well, his teeth are straight now. And his skin isn't all blotchy the way it was when he was in high school, either. And he wears a crew cut, so his hair doesn't stick out like porcupine quills the way it used to."

"Where does he live now?" asked Jean, more from politeness than from interest.

"His family moved up into the hills," answered Sue. "He's going to the University now. He's going to be an entomologist."

"Is that the study of bugs or words?" asked Jean. "I never can remember."

"Insects," answered Sue.

This confirmed Jean's feelings about Old Repulsive. He was exactly the kind of boy she would expect to study insects.

"He talked to me quite a while," said Sue, and added almost shyly, "I think he likes me."

"Do you want him to?" Jean hid her dismay upon realizing that her sister was so eager to have a boy like her that she would snatch at this one.

"Yes," said Sue thoughtfully, "I do."

"I hope he does like you." Jean kept the stiffness she felt out of her voice. How fortunate she was to have a good-looking boy like Johnny like her. There was something pathetic about Sue's eagerness to make Kenneth sound attractive, as if perhaps she wanted to catch up with her younger sister.

The girls heard a car turn into the driveway. Jean, glad to have the disturbing conversation about Old

Repulsive interrupted, got up to set the coffeepot back on the burner to reheat.

"What happened to you?" both girls asked their father, as soon as he opened the back door.

Mr. Jarrett removed the black raincoat and handed it to Sue, who carried it into the bathroom to drip into the tub. "It was that little lady near the end of my route," he said, stooping to pull off his rubbers and to pat Dandy, who had come running, his half a tail wagging, at the sound of his voice.

"The one with the son in New York who never writes?" Jean took a cup and saucer out of the cupboard.

"Yes," answered Mr. Jarrett. "She came out on the porch in this rain to ask if I was positive I didn't have a letter from New York for her. She was so sure she would get one today. She said she had a hunch."

"She says that every day," said Sue, coming out of the bathroom.

"I know." There was regret in Mr. Jarrett's voice, and his daughters knew he would have liked to bring the lady a letter from her son every day. "She was so disappointed that when I got back to the post office I looked around and sure enough, there was a letter for her from New York. Airmail. I got to thinking about this poor woman living all alone and spending the whole weekend wishing she had that letter. So when I left the office I drove out to her house and gave it to her. I wish you could have seen her face when she saw that return address."

Jean and Sue smiled affectionately at their father. "We might have known," said Sue. "Last week it was the lady who was watching for the colored slides of her trip to Europe, because she was having company that evening and wanted to show them."

"And the week before it was the girl watching for

the letter from the sailor in Okinawa," added Jean, pouring a steaming cup of coffee for her father.

"It was a small thing to do, and it made her happy. I only wish it had been a thicker letter." Mr. Jarrett accepted the coffee with a grateful smile for Jean. "Are you ready for that young man of yours?"

"Yes," answered Jean. "Now if the weather will just clear up before tonight."

But by the time Mrs. Jarrett came home from work it was obvious that the storm would not only continue but would probably grow worse. Squalls of wind dashed rain against the living-room and dining-room windows. Rain gurgled down the chimney and plopped into the cold ashes in the fireplace. The branches of the trees that lined the street bowed and lashed and tossed.

"I hope the roof doesn't leak." Mrs. Jarrett sounded worried. Their roof, as they all knew, was old, and although Mr. Jarrett had patched it last summer, it needed reshingling.

Jean began to be uneasy. Perhaps Johnny would not be able to come after all. She listened for cars on the street, and it seemed a very long time before one passed. A branch torn from a tree blew against the house. At the back of her mind was the worry that she was not attractive enough or interesting enough for a boy to come through a storm to see. Don't be silly, she told herself sternly. "Neither rain, nor snow, nor heat, nor gloom of night. . . ." Now she was being even sillier. Johnny was not a mailman.

Jean tried to shut out the fear that the telephone might ring and it would be Johnny breaking the date. She wondered if Elaine and Maxine had had fun marketing for their supper and how many Greek olives they had had money for when everything else had been purchased. She wondered if Elaine missed her and if Maxine liked avocados as much as she did.

When supper was over and the dishes washed, Jean took one last reassuring peek into the refrigerator at the two desserts she had saved for herself and Johnny. So far he had not telephoned to break the date, so maybe everything was going to be all right after all. She went to her room to change her dress.

Sue was already sitting at the table with a pile of books and notes in front of her. "Term paper," she said.

"May I extend my sympathy?" asked Jean, who admired her sister for starting her term paper in the middle of the semester. She changed into her best blouse and a bright cotton skirt. She brushed her hair and carefully arranged her bangs. The rain was still beating against the windows. "Isn't this a terrible night?" she said, wanting and yet not wanting to discuss with Sue the possibility that Johnny might be kept home by the weather.

"Mm-hm," murmured Sue, her head bent over her notebook. A blast of wind seemed to shake the house.

Jean tiptoed out of the room. In the living room she found her father kneeling on the hearth, starting a fire in the fireplace.

"I thought this might be a good time to get rid of some of the cartons and a couple of orange crates that were cluttering up the garage," Mr. Jarrett said. "They won't last long, but I thought a little fire might brighten things up."

"Good idea, Daddy." Jean could not help being touched. This was her father's way of showing that he, too, was pleased that a boy was coming to see one of his daughters. The papers and cartons caught fire, making the room seem more pleasant and the storm less threatening. While Mr. Jarrett broke up the orange crates, Jean sat down on a chair near the front door, got up, and moved to the couch. She did not want Johnny to look through the glass door and see her sitting there as if she couldn't wait to open the door. She looked around the room at the fire, the African violet blooming cheerily on the mantel, the Chinese checker set waiting on the coffee table, and was satisfied. Their house might be small, but it was homelike—tonight one could even call it cozy—and no one would notice the crack in the plaster or the worn places in the carpet. Her father, who was oudoors so much, was better-looking than most men his age and no one would ever guess, looking at her mother, that she had stood on her feet all day selling remnants.

At a quarter to eight Jean walked across the room and straightened a book, just to get a glimpse of herself in the mirror over the mantel. Johhny was right. She was a cute girl. Eight o'clock came. Jean grew tense. Eight-fifteen. Above the sound of the wind and the rain and the gurgling gutters Jean heard a car approach, and pass on down the street. Had Johnny forgotten? Of course not. It was needless to worry when he was only fifteen minutes late. "This is the worst storm we have had this year," Jean observed, laying the ground for excuses in case Johnny really did not come.

Eight-thirty. Jean's mouth was dry and her hands were cold. She longed to say brightly, as if it did not matter, Well, it looks as if Johnny isn't coming. She could not. Not yet. Give him another five minutes. Or ten.

Raindrops hissed into the fire. "Didn't you say this fellow was coming at eight?" asked Mr. Jarrett.

"Yes," said Jean miserably, knowing that her father did not really mean to be tactless. "At least I think that was what he said. I might have misunderstood." The pieces of orange crate burned through, broke apart, fell into coals. When ten more drops hissed into the fire Johnny would come. No, better make it twenty. One . . . two . . .

Mrs. Jarrett looked up from the pad of paper on her knee. "Do you think it would sound all right to say a cold cream leaves your face with a gossamer glow?" she asked.

"Yes, Mother." Jean was not thinking about her mother's question. Johnny had not asked for her address. Perhaps he was in a telephone booth someplace, calling all the Jarretts in the book. How many Jarretts were there, she wondered, and did she dare go look? Her mother's words finally penetrated. "I mean, no," she amended hastily. "Gossamer doesn't glow. At least I don't think it does. I think it would be all right to say gossamer soft but I don't think you can say gossamer glow."

"I guess you are right," said Mrs. Jarrett. "But I do think alliterative phrases stand a better chance of winning." Then, as if the subject had been on her mind all the time, she said, "Don't worry, dear. In a storm like this Johnny could easily be delayed. Perhaps his car won't start."

"Maybe," was all Jean was able to say. Any excuse was better than none. The three sat in silence, listening to the wind and the rain, the sound of burning wood crumbling into coals. Every time Jean heard tires on the street her heart felt like something trying to beat its way out of a cage.

By ten minutes to nine the fire was reduced to hot ashes. That fire had been her father's contribution to her evening, Jean thought sadly. Whatever would she say when Elaine telephoned in the morning? And Elaine would telephone. The very first thing. Jean pictured herself answering the telephone, chattering brightly. Elaine, it was all the most *ghastly* mistake. Ghastly in a *hilarious* sort of way, if you know what I mean. There we sat by those dying embers, listening for a car to stop, and all the time I had the wrong day. Except that she did not have the wrong day and even if she did, she would not talk to Elaine that way. That was the way Elaine talked when she was trying to turn an incident into an event.

Mr. Jarrett yawned.

"I—I guess he isn't coming." With tremendous effort Jean contrived a wry half-smile. "Maybe he was just—joking or something." Maybe that was it. Why should a boy who wore shirts that had to be dry-cleaned want to come to see a girl like her?

Mr. Jarrett was busy poking the dead fire. Mrs. Jarrett bit her lip and looked at Jean, her eyes dark with sympathy—sympathy that Jean appreciated and at the same time resented. Part of her wanted to bury her face in her mother's lap the way she had when she was a little girl, and another part of her wanted to hold her head high and say proudly, I'm fifteen—I can manage my own affairs.

The telephone rang. None of the Jarretts seemed able to move. It rang a second time and a third.

"Answer it, dear," said Mrs. Jarrett, on the fourth ring.

Numbly Jean walked into the kitchen and picked up the receiver.

"Hello, Jean?" It was Johnny all right.

"Oh, hi, Johnny," Jean said in a strangled voice.

"Look, Jean. I'm sure sorry, but I am not going to be able to make it tonight after all." Johnny sounded genuinely contrite.

"That's all right, Johnny." It wasn't all right, but what could a girl say?

"No, it isn't all right," insisted Johnny. "I feel terrible about it. Some people from out of town arrived and Dad says I have to stick around. You know how it is. Old family friends and all."

"Sure, Johnny." Jean felt somewhat better. Johnny

really did sound sorry, and anybody's family could have out-of-town friends arrive. Even on a night like this. Of course they could.

"I'll make it up to you sometime," said Johnny, almost tenderly. "Honest."

"Oh, that's all right," said Jean, beginning to feel that it was all right.

Johnny lowered his voice, as if he did not want anyone to overhear what he was saying. "Jean? Did I ever tell you what a cute little nose you have?"

Jean smiled into the telephone in spite of herself. "No, I don't think so." Unconsciously she lowered her voice too, and enjoyed a delightful sense of conspiracy.

"Remind me on Monday and I'll tell you," said Johnny softly.

Jean laughed. "I'll do that." At least she would get to see him day after tomorrow.

"Look, Jean," said Johnny, his voice still low, "I've got to go now. I'm sure sorry and I'll see you Monday."

"See you Monday," agreed Jean. "And I'm sorry you couldn't make it."

Reluctantly Jean went into the living room to repeat Johnny's conversation, omitting the part about her cute little nose, to her mother and father.

"What a shame," said Mrs. Jarrett mildly.

"It seems to me he could have phoned a little sooner," said Mr. Jarrett.

Jean had tried to ignore this thought.

"We don't know," said Mrs. Jarrett. "Perhaps he couldn't."

"It seems to me if a boy really liked a girl—" began Mr. Jarrett.

"Now, Jim," interrupted Mrs. Jarrett.

"It's all right, Daddy," said Jean earnestly. "Really it is. He said he would make it up to me and he would see me Monday. And he sounded truly sorry."

Mr. Jarrett, who still did not look convinced, changed his manner abruptly. "I'll bet I can still beat my daughter at Chinese checkers," he said jovially.

"No, thank you, Daddy. Not tonight. I—I don't feel like playing." Jean could not play checkers with her father, not after she had planned to play with Johnny. Poor Daddy, his attempt to make her feel better was so sweet and so clumsy, but she did wish he would not try to be understanding. She didn't *need* to feel better, because everything was perfectly all right. There was no reason to make an issue out of Johnny's not being able to come. It wasn't as though he hadn't wanted to come.

Jean stood uncertainly in the doorway, not knowing how to use the remnant of the evening. While she stood there listening to the storm she discovered that she was tired, very tired. "I guess I might as well go to bed," she said.

"Good night, dear," said Mrs. Jarrett gently.

Now Jean had to face Sue, who looked up from her books when Jean opened the door of their room. "Too bad, Jean," said Sue quietly.

"Oh, it's perfectly all right," said Jean, trying to sound vivacious in spite of her weariness. What was wrong with her family that they could not see there was nothing to be sorry about? Why did they have to go around being so sympathetic? They were treating her as if she were an invalid or something. The way they were behaving, they would probably start tiptoeing and speaking in hushed voices—and bringing her dishes of blancmange.

Well, they could just stop being so understanding, Jean thought crossly as she turned back her bedspread. Lots of girls would be glad to have Johnny look forward to seeing them on Monday. To have Johnny make a date was something, even if he did have to break it. Jean walked over to the mirror and studied her nose. Johnny was right. It was a cute little nose. She wondered why she had never thought so before. And her family could just stop being so horribly understanding.

CHAPTER
5

Although Jean had made up her mind that this was one Monday when she would not wait for Johnny after school, not for more than two seconds, anyway, she was overjoyed to find that Johnny was as good as his word. He arrived at the door of the sewing room almost as soon as the bell had rung, and after looking inside this feminine precinct, he actually entered, causing all the girls who were putting away their sewing boxes or finishing seams on the sewing machines to look up. Boys did not often venture into the clothing class.

Jean was so flustered she dropped her thimble. This would show her horribly sympathetic family, when she happened to mention it at the dinner table! "This afternoon when Johnny came into the sewing room to find me," she would begin.

"He's *darling*," whispered Mitsuko, as Jean bent to pick up the thimble. "You're lucky."

Undisturbed by the stir he was creating, Johnny made his way to Jean's table, where she was stuffing her tape measure and spools of thread into her sewing box with trembling hands.

"Hi," said Johnny, looking down at Jean.

"Hi," answered Jean, coloring because she felt as conspicuous as if she were on a stage. She stowed her sewing box in her drawer and shoved the drawer shut.

"I always wondered what went on in here," remarked Johnny.

"And now you know," said Jean lightly, and smiled up at him.

Johnny put his hand on her elbow (actually put his hand on her elbow!) and walked with her out of the sewing room while the other girls watched. "Did I ever tell you you have a cute little nose?" Johnny asked softly.

"I believe you may have mentioned it at some time or another." Jean felt that her conversation was improving rapidly. Dear, charming Johnny. However, she was puzzled by an uneasy feeling that she had lost or forgotten something. For a moment she could not think what it was and then it came to her. She had not forgotten anything at all. Homer was missing. "Where's your friend?" she asked.

"He got lost," said Johnny briefly.

Jean did not pursue the subject, because she was not really interested in what had happened to Homer. She was so happy to have Johnny all to herself for a change and she was more interested in her nose than in Homer. Johnny not only walked out of the building with her but accompanied her to the bus stop, waited in the crowd for her bus to arrive, and then waved to her after she had climbed on the bus and paid her fare. Just wait until she told her sympathetic family! As Johnny said, when he waited for the bus with me. . . .

Except for Thursday, when Johnny and several other boys made the tape recording of the Hi-times program to be broadcast Saturday morning, Johnny met Jean and accompanied her to the bus stop every day that week. He was always interesting to talk to.

He told Jean more about his experiences skiing and about the time he became entangled in seaweed while skin diving off Point Lobos.

On Friday Jean waited expectantly for Johnny to say something about a date, but he did not. She realized there was no reason why she should not invite him to come to her house Saturday evening. Probably that was what she should do, since he might still be embarrassed because he had been forced to break the date with her. "Johnny," she began as the bus pulled up to the curb, but she was caught in the crowd that surged toward the door of the bus.

"Were you going to say something?" Johnny called.

"No," Jean called back, over her shoulder. "I mean—good-by." A girl could not very well yell an invitation to a boy from the steps of a bus. Disheartened, Jean paid her fare and was lucky enough to get a seat. Three other students not so fortunate promptly piled their books on her lap, and from beneath the books Jean reflected on her disappointment. She also reflected ruefully that she had spent more money on carfare that week than she had intented to, but when a boy walked her to her bus stop and waited for the bus with her, she could not very well tell him that she walked home whenever she could, to save carfare.

When Jean reached her house and was changing from her school clothes, she looked gloomily at her books on the study table and wondered if she could be noble and get her homework out of the way now, or leave it until Sunday evening. This was a question she considered every Friday after school. Sue, who was always prompt and efficient, would do most of hers today, she knew, but she was not Sue. She liked to postpone her homework as long as possible, in spite of all the sensible arguments for doing it promptly.

While Jean was debating with herself (go on, get it out of the way so you can forget it; no, I don't feel like doing it now, because I would rather think about Johnny), Sue came home from school and walked into the bedroom with a large brown-paper bundle which she dropped on her bed.

"What's that?" asked Jean, pulling up the zipper on her skirt. She would have preferred a button and buttonhole on the waistband instead of hooks and eyes, but she had not come to buttonholes yet in her clothing class.

"The Jarrett sisters seek their fortunes! We don't need any long-lost uncle." Sue seemed unusually gay as she pulled the string off the bundle and laid back the paper, revealing a quantity of fabric in two colors, red and turquoise-blue.

Jean leaned over and fingered the material, which she found to be a heavy rayon crepe, scarcely appropriate for dresses and certainly not suitable for drapes or bedspreads. "What in the world are you going to do with all that material in those colors?" asked Jean. "There must be enough to slipcover an elephant."

"That material," said Sue, "represents our fortunes." She sat down on the bed and held a length of red material against her cheek, as if she enjoyed the feel of it. "We are going to make stoles for the *a cappella* choir to wear over their dark-blue robes."

"Us?" said Jean. "But we aren't in the choir."

"We don't have to be." Sue went on to explain. "You see, the choir needs new stoles, and anybody in Advanced Clothing who wants to can make them. Not many of the girls in the class were interested, but I thought it would be a wonderful chance to earn some money—they will pay us a dollar and a quarter apiece—and so I brought home a pile of the material and a pattern. They aren't hard to make. They are red, with a turquoise edging two inches wide on the inside edge. The hardest part will be getting the edging straight, but I know you can do it if you baste."

"Why, Sue, that's almost too good to be true!" Jean rapidly calculated that four stoles equaled five dollars. "How many do they need?"

"Over a hundred. Tall, medium, and short," answered Sue. "My teacher said when I finished this material I can take home some more."

"And Daddy can't possibly object," Jean pointed out. "Come on, what are we waiting for? Let's go to work!"

Her homework held at bay for a while and her disappointment over Johnny temporarily out of her mind, Jean enjoyed spreading the bright material on the table, pinning on the brown wrapping-paper pattern, and cutting with long slashes of the scissors. She picked up an unsewn stole and buried her nose in it. "Mmm," she breathed. "I just love the smell of new material."

"So do I," said Sue from the closet, where she was getting out the portable sewing machine. "I wish someone would bottle it for perfume, so I could dab it behind my ears."

Jean pinned the shoulder seams of a stole. "What would you name the perfume?" she mused. "Silken Scent?"

"No, I don't think so," said Sue, as if the matter was of great importance. "I think I would name it after a fabric. Crepe de Chine would make a good name. Or Peau de Soie."

Jean giggled. "We sound like Mother working on a contest."

Sue lifted the sewing machine from its case and set it on the table. "Who knows? Maybe Mother will run across a perfume-naming contest and we can offer her our prize-winning suggestions. She has thought up names for almost everything else. Why not perfume?"

The evening passed quickly for both girls, and by bedtime Jean had the satisfaction of having earned three dollars and seventy-five cents with her two hands. Sue, who was not afraid to make the old sewing machine roar down the length of a seam, had completed four stoles and cut out two more.

On Saturday morning, after they had finished their household chores, Jean and Sue continued sewing on the stoles. They cut, pinned, basted, and stitched until their room was a tangle of color.

"Do you think we could say the money we earn is stolen money?" asked Sue.

"That is practically the worst pun I have ever heard," said Jean, and laughed. Four stoles equaled five dollars or a new slip, a pretty blouse, material for a cotton dress. Eight stoles equaled a ten-dollar bill, something Jean almost never had in her possession. There were so many things a girl could do with ten dollars. With luck, and a sale, she could buy a ready-made cotton dress, a dress that was not cut out by a pattern that had to be altered for a girl who was shorter than average. Jean was rapt in the limitless possibilities of a ten-dollar bill, when the doorbell rang. "I'll get it," she said, because Sue was using the sewing machine.

When Jean opened the front door she found Johnny standing on the porch. "Why, Johnny!" She could not keep her surprise from showing.

Johnny grinned engagingly. "I was just cruising around and I wondered if you would like to go down to the drive-in for a Coke?"

"Now?" Jean still could not quite believe that Johnny was really standing on her doorstep.

"Sure," said Johnny. "Why not?"

"Why not?" agreed Jean, delighted. "Just a minute. I'll get my sweater." She was quite sure her father would not object to her going to the drive-in in the daytime.

In the bedroom, Jean whispered, "It's Johnny! He wants me to go to the drive-in for a Coke!" Oh, the joy of saying Johnny wanted her to do something!

"At quarter of ten in the morning?" Sue did not sound entirely approving.

"Sure. Why not?" Jean snatched her sweater and jerked a comb through her bangs.

"Have fun," said Sue.

"I shall," answered Jean, almost defiantly. It was too bad there were not two Johnnies, one for each of them, but that was the way things were. They couldn't all be lucky.

Jean and Johnny walked down the steps to the Volkswagen in the driveway. "I've always wanted to ride in one of these little cars," Jean told Johnny, as he held the door open for her.

"This is Mom's car," he said. "She keeps it for a pet." Johnny folded his long legs into the small car and backed it down the driveway. "It doesn't really have a motor. It's powered by a gnome turning an egg beater. It's much cheaper than gas."

"And here I thought that noise coming from the back of the car instead of the front was the engine," said Jean, "and all the time it was an egg beater. What do you feed the gnome? A saucer of milk, or is that just for brownies?"

"This gnome likes Cokes and French fries," answered Johnny.

Jean basked in being alone with Johnny, but when he drove into the parking area of the drive-in and brought the car to a halt between two white lines, Jean felt as if she had run out of conversation. Too shy to look at Johnny, she read the signs posted on the front of the drive-in. "Jumboburgers—1/4 lb. beef on bun 37¢." "French fries 14¢." "Porkchopettes 79¢."

"Two Cokes," Johnny yelled out the window, to the carhop who was approaching. She smiled, nodded, and turned back. Johnny glanced at his watch. "We're just in time," he remarked, and turned on the radio.

"Time for what?" asked Jean.

"Hi-times," he said. "Don't you listen?"

"Every Saturday," answered Jean, embarrassed that the actual presence of Johnny had made her forget the program.

The theme song and then Johnny's voice came out of the loud-speaker. "Good morning. This is Johnny Chessler, your Hi-times announcer broadcasting by tape-recording from the control room of Northgate High School." Johnny listened intently.

Jean listened too, relieved of the burden of conversation. Now she had a chance to think about what she wanted to say to Johnny when the program ended. She wanted to talk to him, to find out more about him, and most of all, to learn the answer to the question that had fascinated her since December. Why had he asked her to dance with him? This was her opportunity if she could only manipulate the conversation. It was too bad she couldn't have a script writer, like the Hi-times program.

When the carhop set the tray on the car door beside Johnny, Jean accepted a Coke from Johnny and silently sipped it through the straw. There really was no reason why she couldn't come right out and ask Johnny about that evening at the clubhouse.

"Now that the cast of the variety show has been chosen and rehearsals will start next week," said Johnny's voice, "committees have been appointed to start the ball rolling on another event on the social calendar of Northgate High School—the Girls' Association Dance, which will be held on the eleventh of April, in the gymnasium. Hawaiian Holiday is the theme, and this time the girls invite the boys. Smile for the ladies, boys, and maybe you will be lucky enough to get an invitation." Johnny listened to every word.

And probably half the girls in school will ask
Johnny to go to that dance, thought Jean unhappily.
There was no use even thinking about it herself—she
knew she would never have the courage. She stirred
the ice in her Coke with her straw and told herself, I'll
just say casually, Johnny, do you remember that night
at the clubhouse when you asked me to dance? And he
will say, Yes, Jean, what about it? And I'll say, How
did you happen to ask me to dance when I was so obviously not a part of the crowd? Or maybe she
shouldn't ask. Maybe it would be better not to recall
the episode at all.

Jean sipped her Coke slowly, trying to make it last,
while she listened to Johnny's voice on the radio and
stole glances at Johnny himself, absorbed in his own
words. He had such a regular profile and was so attractive with his curls tumbling over his forehead that
way. And it was pleasant to hear Johnny's voice coming out of the loud-speaker instead of Johnny, because
she was spared the anxiety of conversation, of wondering if she had said the right thing, of weighing the
meaning of Johnny's words. Yes, this was a pleasant
moment, sitting in a car in the drive-in sipping a Coke
as if she came to this popular spot every day. She
could not help marveling that the words she was hearing had been spoken by Johnny on Thursday, re-
corded on tape, preserved for two days, and were now
being played from a radio station. Gradually she, too,
became engrossed in the sound of Johnny's voice. As
the words flowed by, Jean ceased to listen to their
meaning and listened only to the stream of pleasant
sound. Then his voice stopped to allow the playing of
a record.

"Oh, Johnny!" exclaimed Jean, turning toward him.
"You sound marvelous!"

"You really think so?" Obviously Johnny was
pleased by her admiration.

"Oh, yes," said Jean. "With your voice you should be an announcer or an actor."

"I do the best I can with the scripts the literary club writes." Johnny frowned slightly. "The trouble is, they don't realize some of the problems of radio broadcasting, so I've got to learn to be more careful with my enunciation in phrases like 'Girls' Association.' Those *s*'s made too much of a hissing sound," he said critically.

"Nobody would ever notice," said Jean.

The record ended. Johnny interviewed the drama coach, who said he thought this variety show was going to be one of the best Northgate High had ever staged. When the program was over, Johnny turned to Jean. "Like it?" he asked.

"Oh, yes," said Jean. "You were every bit as good as a professional announcer and better than lots of them."

Johnny grinned. "Did I ever tell you you are cute?"

Johnny's voice issuing from Johnny's mouth was much more satisfactory after all, even though Jean did not know how to answer. If she said yes it would sound as if she treasured his casual remarks—which she did, but was not going to let him know it. And if she said no, it would sound as if she were seeking compliments—which she longed to do. Instead of answering, she looked down at her Coke and smiled.

"Did you know you have dimples when you smile like that?" asked Johnny.

"Have I?" Jean decided this was a good moment to risk asking the question. "Is that why you asked me to dance that night at the Christmas party?"

Johnny laughed. "Partly, I guess. You looked so cute and eager, sitting there watching."

Jean stored this away to mull over at her leisure. "I thought I looked terrible in my saddle shoes and that awful plaid skirt," she said, laughing lightly. "I had been helping with some decorations for a party the next day, so I wasn't dressed up." She handed Johnny her empty Coke glass to set on the tray. Johnny did not need to know that it was Elaine's mother's party and not her own.

Johnny looked searchingly at Jean as if he were memorizing the features. Jean was both flattered and flustered. "I know I must have been terrible to dance with." She forced a gay laugh. "But I have improved a lot since then. I have had some practice." It certainly would not hurt to let him know that she had learned to dance since that night. Never mind how she had learned. A girl did not have to tell a boy everything.

The carhop removed the tray from the car door, depriving them of the right to occupy one of the drive-in's parking spaces, even though the lot was almost empty at that hour in the morning. When Johnny started the car and headed toward her house, Jean was disappointed, because she had hoped they might drive around for a while. She considered saying it was such a beautiful spring day that it must be possible to see for miles from the hills, but rejected the remark as being too obvious. When Johnny let her out of the car and walked her to the front door, she asked, "Won't you come in?"

"No, thanks. Not this time," he said, smiling down at her. "I have to be getting home. Mom needs the car."

This time! That meant there would be a next time. "Well—thanks for the Coke." Jean was reluctant to let Johnny go. "And it was fun listening to the program."

Johnny smiled at Jean as if he were amused in an affectionate sort of way. "See you around," he said, and was gone.

Jean closed the door and watched from the window while Johnny backed down the driveway. She had had a date with Johnny! And she had found out what she wanted to know. It was true that she was a little disappointed that he had brought her home so soon and had not asked her for another date, but. . . . Oh, well, there was always next week. Humming *Play Like You Love Me*, she walked into the bedroom.

"Back so soon?" asked Sue, as she silenced the roar of the sewing machine.

"Johnny had to take the car back. His mother needed it," Jean explained, as she dropped her sweater on the foot of the bed.

"Oh." The sewing machine began to race down the length of a seam again.

Jean stood in front of the mirror that hung over the chest of drawers she shared with Sue, and looked thoughtfully at herself. She looked down, smiled demurely the way she had smiled for Johnny in the car, and tried to peek out from beneath her lashes to see how she had looked to Johnny.

"What are you looking like that for?" asked Sue curiously.

Jean had not noticed that the sewing machine had stopped once more. "Was I looking any special way?" she asked innocently, as she turned from the mirror. It was unfortunate that a girl could not have one shred of privacy in her own home. She sat down, picked up a stole, started to baste, discovered she was basting a long facing to a short stole, and put her work down again. She felt too restless to settle down to sewing.

"There," said Sue, folding a finished stole and glancing at the clock on the table between the two beds. "I think I'll stop for now. I have to go downtown."

"What for?" asked Jean, knowing Sue did not spend carfare unnecessarily.

"I need some more material from the main library for my term paper," explained Sue. "I just received a reserve card saying the book I tried to get last week is in now."

When Jean had the house to herself she felt an unaccustomed freedom. She seized an armful of red and turquoise material and threw it into the air just for the joy of watching it fall in a brilliant heap upon her bed. Johnny, Johnny, Johnny, she thought. She brushed and combed her hair as meticulously as if she expected Johnny to ring the doorbell at any moment. She wandered into the kitchen and opened the refrigerator, to see what she could find for her lunch. It was early for lunch, but she could not think of anything else to do. She stared dreamily at the covered dishes of leftovers, the cartons of milk, a tomato-juice can half full of bacon fat, and wished they all would turn into avocados, artichokes, and delicious little tea-party sandwiches. They did not, so she poured herself a glass of milk and made a peanut-butter sandwich. She was scarcely aware of what she was eating.

When Jean finished her lunch she could not think of anything she wanted to do. She reread the headlines of the morning paper, but wars and labor unions and bills before Congress were too remote from her springtime mood. She turned on the television set and got an exercise program that happened to be on. "Come on, girls, let's get up off those chairs and firm our thighs," directed a muscular young man. "Right hand on hip, swing your left leg out to the side. One, two. One, two. That's right. One, two. One, two." Jean halfheartedly slimmed her thighs for a few measures of organ music before she turned the set off again.

Feeling that Sue was lucky to have an excuse for going downtown to the library, Jean was seized by a desire to leave the house, to be out in the sunshine. Maybe she didn't have any reason to go to the library downtown, but she could walk to the branch library to do some reference work for her history class. Jean picked up her notebook and, followed by Dandy, left the house, but even as she tried the door to make sure it was locked she knew that she would not do any work when she reached the library. The walk was pleasant, however, for her thoughts were filled with Johnny.

At the library Jean did pause beside the encyclopedias long enough to think how much she did not want to open one of those heavy volumes today. She wandered into the periodical section and thumbed through the fashion magazines. How wonderful it must be to be as tall as a fashion model and to wear, even for a little while, such lovely clothes: evening gowns, slim suits, hats like flower gardens. None of these was meant for her, but in the back of one of the magazines, in a section called "Important Clothes for Little Money," Jean found a photograph of a saucy-looking model wearing a dress she longed to own. The full skirt was gathered onto a simple waist that had a little round collar and buttons down the front. The fabric was pink, printed with clover blossoms in a deeper shade, and there must have been five yards in the skirt alone. The price was forty-nine dollars and ninety-five cents. And they call that little money, thought Jean. To her, forty-nine dollars and ninety-five cents seemed like a fortune. It was—let's see— forty a *cappella* choir stoles.

Then, because Jean did not really want to be in the library at all, she returned the magazine to the rack and, mentally wearing the clover dress, she started homeward, followed by Dandy, who had napped on the library steps. What she really wanted more than anything was to talk to Johnny again, and as she walked, her imaginary skirt silken against her legs, she looked up at the trees, which had shed their blossoms and were now putting forth sweet green foliage and

thought, Why not? She would have the house to herself. All she had to do was make up an excuse to telephone him. Why shouldn't she hear his voice once?
Maybe if she talked to him, he would ask to come
over. It took Jean only a moment to hit upon an excuse for telephoning Johnny. She would hear his voice
in person, over the telephone, and on the radio—all in
one day! She lived in a wonderful age indeed.

As soon as Jean unlocked the front door, she
dropped her notebook on a table and went straight to
the telephone. She did not need to look up Johnny's
telephone number. She knew it as well as she knew the
license number of his father's car. With a trembly finger she dialed Toyon 1-4343 and waited, with her
heart thumping, for Johnny to answer.

After the second ring a woman's voice said, "Hello?"

Jean had been so preoccupied with Johnny that she
was unprepared for this woman's voice.

"Hello?" the woman repeated impatiently. In the
background Jean heard Johnny call, "Hey, Mom!"

Silently Jean replaced the receiver. She could not
bring herself to ask for Johnny. Then, annoyed with
herself, she sat biting at her thumb and wondering
why she had been so foolish. There was no reason why
she should not ask to speak to Johnny. No reason at
all. Now that she knew he was home she would try
again after a decent interval—say about five minutes—
and if his mother answered a second time, she would
calmly ask if she might speak to Johnny.

In exactly five minutes or three hundred seconds by
the clock, Jean dialed again. In Johnny's house the
telephone rang and rang and rang again. Jean tried to
picture how it looked, in the kitchen or on a table in
the hall, calling angrily for someone to come and lift
the receiver. Or perhaps in a such a large house there
were two telephones, both of them demanding to be

answered. Five rings. Six rings. The receiver was lifted! Jean thought her heart would stop.

"Hello?" It was the woman's impatient voice again.

"May I please speak to Johnny?" asked Jean.

"Just a moment." Mrs. Chessler, if that was who she was, spoke crisply.

"Hello?" Johnny's voice at last.

"Oh—hello, Johnny. This is Jean." Somehow Jean got the words out, even though she did not seem to have the breath with which to speak them.

"Oh, hi, Jean." Johnny sounded casual, friendly, and not at all surprised to hear her voice.

"Johnny, I was wondering—" began Jean. "I was wondering—if I left my sweater in your car. I mean— I thought I took it with me and now I can't find it any-place. I've looked everywhere, and well, it just occurred to me I might have put it over the back of the seat and it could have fallen back onto the floor."

"Hold on a minute, Jean," said Johnny, "and I'll go out to the garage and have a look."

"All right, Johnny," Jean waited, feeling the beat of her own heart. Had there been a note, a grace note, of amusement in Johnny's voice?

"Hello, Jean." Johnny was on the line again. "Sorry. It isn't there, and Mom says she didn't see it when she took the car out a little while ago."

"Oh, dear," said Jean. "I wonder what I could have done with it. I've looked everywhere."

"I'm afraid I can't help you," answered Johnny.

Was that impatience in his voice, too? Jean could hear the sound of a faucet running and the rattle of pans, telling her that Johnny's telephone was in the kitchen. Jean waited a moment for Johnny to say something—any little remark that could prolong the conversation—but she heard only the rush of water.

"Well, thanks a lot, Johnny," Jean was forced to say

when the silence had stretched to an awkward length. "Sorry I had to bother you."

"That's all right, Jean," said Johnny.

"Good-by, Johnny."

"Good-by."

As Jean sat for a moment with her hand on the telephone she clung to that last word, letting it ring through her mind so she could examine every inflection, every nuance, in those two syllables. Impatience was there, she was quite certain, but naturally a boy would not want to have a long conversation with a girl when his mother was in the same room. Although Jean tried to persuade herself that this was true, she knew with a terrible certainty that she had made a mistake. She had not fooled Johnny one bit and, what was worse, she had not been able to keep wistfulness out of her voice. Johnny sounded perfectly friendly, and she could have lost her sweater, couldn't she? Yes, but she had not. In her heart Jean knew that Johnny had seen through her maneuver.

That was that. With a sigh of regret Jean decided that she might as well spend the rest of the afternoon sewing on *a cappella* choir stoles. Next time—if there was a next time—she would know better. She left the telephone and went to the bedroom, where she was startled to see Sue lying on her bed, with her head propped up on her hand, reading a book. "Oh—hello, Sue," she said, realizing that Sue must have overheard her telephone call. "I didn't know you were home."

"I ran into Ken Cory at the library and he gave me a ride home," said Sue. She looked levelly at Jean and said, "Your sweater is lying on your bed."

"Why, so it is!" Jean tried to cover up her feelings by picking up the stole she had been basting together. "I could have sworn I had lost it."

Sue sat up and closed her book. "Jean," she said. "Please don't."

Jean moistened her fingertip and tied a knot in her thread. "Please don't what?" she asked, although she knew very well what Sue was talking about.

"Please don't chase Johnny." There was real concern in Sue's voice.

That concern put Jean on the defensive. "I'm not chasing him," she said, and her voice was cool.

"Oh, Jean!" exclaimed Sue. "Who do you think you are fooling, phoning a boy on such a made-up excuse?"

Jean flung the stole on her bed. "Is there anything so terrible about phoning a boy?" she demanded. "Is there?"

"No, there isn't anything so terrible about it," said Sue, "but I don't think it was the thing to do when you didn't really have a reason to phone him."

"*You* don't think it was the thing to do! Just because you are two years older you think you know everything." Jean did not like the sound of her own voice. She did not want to quarrel with Sue, especially when Sue was right; but that, for some obscure reason, was exactly why she was quarreling. "And what about you? You probably went to the library this morning hoping to meet that awful Kenneth Cory."

Sue lowered her eyes an instant, just long enough to tell Jean her guess was right. "Hoping to meet a boy and telephoning him are not the same," said Sue. "And anyway, Ken had spent the whole morning in the library, hoping I might come in again. He said so. And he isn't awful. He's a whole lot nicer than that Johnny Chessler."

"He isn't either," protested Jean. "Johnny is the nicest boy I know."

"Did he make a date with you?" asked Sue.

"Well, no, not this time," admitted Jean.

"Ken is coming over this evening to take me to the movies," said Sue quietly, "and what is more, I expect he will really get here."

Jean had no answer for this. Both girls sewed in silence in the small bedroom, which seemed stifled by their hot words. Their house was not large enough to hold a quarrel.

Jean mulled the argument over in her mind. It seemed as if suddenly everything she did or said was wrong. First she had made the mistake of telephoning Johnny, and now she was calling the boy her sister liked awful. She felt mixed-up and miserable, and she did not know what to do about it. Couldn't Sue see what a desirable boy Johnny was and how much all the girls admired him?

"Sue," ventured Jean at last, "don't you like Johnny at all?"

"Jean, can't you see?" Sue sounded almost sad. "Johnny just isn't good enough for you."

"Why, how can you say that?" demanded Jean. "Practically every girl in school likes Johnny. I'm the one that isn't good enough."

"Jean, don't think that way about yourself," begged Sue. "You are much too nice to be satisfied with . . . crumbs from a boy like Johnny. I don't know how to say it exactly, but Johnny—oh, I don't know. Maybe we better just forget it." She looked miserable too, as she bent over a stole.

"Johnny what?" persisted Jean.

"Well, for example," said Sue. "One day in English he told Miss Pritchard that he didn't see any reason for wasting his time on trivial assignments."

"Maybe Miss Pritchard's assignments are trivial," said Jean. "Maybe he was right."

"He doesn't get A's. Anyway, it wasn't just that," said Sue unhappily. She put down her sewing and looked pleadingly at Jean. "Don't you see—he doesn't really like you."

"He does like me," said Jean stiffly. Or he had

liked her before she had made the mistake of telephoning him. "I know he does."

"How do you know?" asked Sue.

"He—he expects to see me after school every day,"
said Jean.

"You mean you hang around the halls hoping he
will come by," said Sue. "Naturally he is flattered.
What boy wouldn't be?"

"He always says, 'Hi, how's the cute girl?' And—"

Sue interrupted. "He says that to all the girls. He
even says it to me."

It immediately became urgent for Jean to prove that
Johnny really did like her. "And he said that night at
the clubhouse dance, when Elaine and I were sitting
there, that he asked me to dance because I looked so
cute and eager."

"In other words you looked as if you were asking,
'How much is that doggie in the window?'" said Sue.
"And Johnny gave the little girl a break."

This stung Jean. "Well, I don't care. He does like
me. I know he does. And I am going to ask him to go
to the Girls' Association Dance with me. So there!" Instantly Jean regretted her last two words. It was such a
childish phrase, one that she and Sue had often used in
disagreements when they were little girls. On second
thought Jean regretted the whole rash statement.

Sue jerked at a basting thread. "Go ahead and ask
him," she said, "but he won't go with you."

"Yes, he will." Jean sounded much more positive
than she felt.

Sue unreeled an arm's length of thread from a spool.
"If you really want to take him to the dance," she said
slowly, "I hope he goes with you. Maybe I am wrong,
but I don't think so. And I don't like quarreling."

"Neither do I." Jean went to the sewing machine to
stitch a stole. It would be difficult to talk while the
sewing machine was running, and right now she did

not feel like talking. She slipped one end of the stole
under the foot of the machine, dropped the foot, and
began to stitch. While the machine hummed she found
that in her thoughts she was still arguing with Sue. She
explained to Sue that Johnny really did like her. It
wasn't easy to put into words, but she could tell in
little ways—the way he looked at her, the way he always, or almost always, left the building by the door
nearest the sewing room. And he didn't have to do
that, did he? There were at least six exits from the
building, weren't there? So you see. The advantage of
an imaginary conversation was that the person argued
with did not have the opportunity to advance any un-
welcome points to support his side of the debate. Jean
could always win an imaginary debate.

When Jean finished stitching her seam she glanced
at her sister, who was basting another turquoise edging
to a stole. Sue was frowning slightly, as if her thoughts
were on something more serious than basting together
two pieces of rayon crepe. I'll bet she is going right on
with the argument too, thought Jean wryly.

The girls sewed silently, and while they sewed Jean
thought, Johnny, Johnny, please go to the dance with
me, even if I was foolish enough to phone you on a
flimsy fibbing excuse. He had to accept. He could not
turn her down, not after this conversation with Sue.

But first Jean, who was no longer sure Johnny liked
her, had to find the courage to ask him.

CHAPTER
6

Jean spent an uncomfortable weekend. Her argument with Sue hung in the air like a threatening cloud on a bright day, spoiling their pleasure in working together on the choir stoles. After supper Jean continued to sew alone, but sharing a room with Sue forced her to watch Sue's blithe preparations for her first date. She could not understand Sue's attitude, which was serene as well as happy. Sue knew exactly what she wanted to wear, and she had no trouble getting her lipstick on. One would think she went out with a boy every night of the week. When Jean could not bear to watch Sue another moment, she gathered up her basting thread and material and took them into the living room. Sue would probably be glad to have the bedroom to herself, and Jean could duck out of sight before Ken came. She did not know why, but she did not want to meet her sister's friend.

Jean was so gnawed by the fear that Johnny might be angry with her for telephoning him, and so worried that she might not have the courage to ask him to go to the dance with her and that he might refuse her if she did ask him, that she lost track of time and was surprised when the doorbell rang.

"Answer it, somebody," Sue called.

Because Kenneth could see her through the glass door, there was nothing for Jean to do but put down her sewing and open the door for him.

"Why, hello, Jean!" Kenneth's voice was deeper than she had remembered.

"Won't you come in?" asked Jean. "Sue will be ready in a minute."

"I haven't seen you since you were a little girl," remarked Kenneth, as he stepped into the living room. "You've grown so much that I am not sure I would have known you if I'd seen you on the street."

Kenneth could not have said anything that would have pleased Jean more. While he spoke to Mrs. Jarrett and shook hands with Mr. Jarrett, Jean folded her sewing and at the same time appraised this boy her sister liked. Sue was right. He wasn't awful at all. The ugly duckling had turned into . . . not exactly a swan, but a young man with poise. He seemed grown-up, compared to the boys at school, and although he was not handsome, or even particularly good-looking—there were still some scars on his face from the skin trouble he had had when he was younger—his face was agreeable because it was so . . . What *was* the word? Kind, perhaps. Or gentle. But strong, too. He was genuinely glad to see all of Sue's family, and when Sue entered the room and he helped her on with her coat, Jean thought he acted as if her sister was someone precious to him. And Sue . . . the way she glowed when she looked at Kenneth. . . .

As soon as Sue and Kenneth had gone, Jean did the only thing a girl could possibly do when her sister had a date, and she was left at home worrying for fear the boy she liked was angry with her. She went into the bedroom, muffled her face in her pillow, and had a good cry. Then she dried her eyes and sewed furiously on *a cappella* choir stoles the rest of the evening.

The first thing Monday morning, Jean managed to just happen to meet Johnny in the hall. "Why, *hello*, Johnny," she said, registering great surprise.

"How's the cute girl?" asked Johnny, with his lazy grin.

Did he really say this to all the girls? "I'm fine except—"

"Except what?" asked Johnny.

"Johnny—you aren't mad at me or anything, are you?" Jean began bravely, determined to get at least one of her worries out of the way this morning.

"Mad at you?" Johnny leaned against a locker and looked down at Jean. "What for?"

"For—telephoning you about my sweater." Jean carefully examined the corner of her notebook, which was beginning to fray. "I mean—I thought I had lost it and I thought it would be all right to phone you. I—I just hoped I didn't make you mad or anything."

"Why should I be mad?" Johnny sounded amused. "What was wrong with that?"

"Nothing, I guess, only I thought you sounded sort of—oh, I don't know. Funny." Jean realized she was saying too much. She could have been mistaken about the tone of his voice over the telephone. Maybe he had not been impatient after all. It would be a graver mistake to accuse him now.

"Funny little girl." Johnny sounded almost affectionate.

"I just didn't want you to be mad or anything. I mean—" Oh, *shut up*, Jean told herself. She should stop trying to say what she meant. Babbling on like this was only making things worse. She smiled up at Johnny. "It was nothing, really. I guess I was just imagining things. Well, I have to hurry or I'll be late for English." So *that* was all right, she thought, and found her heart was not as light as she had hoped it would be. She would consider the significance of the phrase "funny little girl" later, when she had time. Now her next problem was to find courage to ask Johnny to go to the dance.

Before Jean found that courage she was swept into the activities of the Costume Club. She attended rehearsals of the variety show and watched acts being pruned and altered to fit the theme "Through the Years." Indians war-whooped, cowboys gathered around a wastebasket to sing campfire songs, colonial ladies and gentlemen in modern school clothes danced the minuet. The Dance Club, whose members had studied modern and ballet dancing, had trouble deciding what they should do; they felt that anyone could do a square dance, and their talent should be used for something more unusual. They argued with one another and with Mr. Kohler, the director, until a member of the stage crew, a muscular type who could not see why a bunch of girls had to make such a fuss about a dance, said in obvious disgust, "Aw, go haunt a house."

The girls decided that haunting a house was exactly what they would do. The art department could design a set that suggested a crumbling Victorian mansion and a few moss-hung trees, and they would compose a bat dance. Still better, at the first of the act, the lights would be bright and some of the girls in Victorian dresses would perform a dance that suggested a game of croquet. Then they would dance off, the lighting would gradually grow dim and eerie (some blue spotlights should do it), and the bats would flit out of the wings to haunt the house.

Because Jean was new to the club and had no particular duties at first, she sat in one of the front rows of the auditorium near the orchestra pit, where, to her amusement, Homer was engrossed in a book, oblivious to the rehearsal when not actually playing his violin. The members of the cast began to ask her to hold their valuables while they rehearsed their act and Jean found herself guarding a lapful of wallets and purses. No sooner had the minuet group finished and col-

lected its belongings from her lap, than the Charleston
dancers dumped their valuables upon her. Jean did
not mind. It was such fun to be participating, even in
this small way, that she wondered why she had not
thought of joining a club before. She now felt as if she
were a part of the school, and not just a girl who attended classes.

And through it all, Johnny, the narrator's script in
his hand, was present. "Testing. One, two, three. Testing." He spoke frequently into the microphone, and
his voice filled the auditorium.

Elaine, too, was part of the crowd. Unfortunately,
Mr. Kohler decided that a boys' war dance would
make a more effective opening for the show and assigned the girls who had planned to do the hoop dance
the part of Indian maidens who stood on papier-
mâché rocks and watched the dance. After rehearsing
her motionless part, Elaine walked down off the stage
and dropped into the seat beside Jean. "Howl!" she
said, raising her arm in an Indian salute.

"How!" answered Jean.

"I'm frustrated by my role," Elaine said, in a world-
weary voice. "There is no scope for my talents just
standing there like Minnehaha or somebody, on that
lover's leap by the shores of the shining big sea water
or whatever it is supposed to be."

"Too bad. All you have to do is look at boys," said
Jean wickedly. "And aren't you thinking of Old No-
komis?"

"The boys are a consolation," agreed Elaine, "but
the trouble is, they don't look at me. And speaking of
boys, have you asked him yet?" Elaine had heard
about Jean's dilemma on the way to school.

Jean looked at Johnny, standing in front of the curtain with his script in hand. He looked so attractive
and so important that she wondered how a mere wal-

let holder would ever find the courage to offer him an invitation. "No," she admitted.

"Don't put it off too long," cautioned Elaine. "You don't want some other girl to grab him. Well, I've got to run. Mom is expecting me."

A fat and battered wallet slid from Jean's lap and disappeared under the seat ahead of her. She piled the rest of the purses and wallets on the seat that Elaine had vacated and got down on her hands and knees to pick up the wallet, which was so stuffed with bits of paper, small change, a comb, and a lipstick that its snap had popped open. As Jean picked up the wallet and started to close it, she could not help noticing a plastic-protected snapshot inside. Still kneeling on the floor, she paused, unable to stop herself, to look at the picture, which was dog-eared beneath the plastic, as if it had been held in a girl's hand many times. It was a snapshot of a boy sitting on some wide steps—the steps of a school, perhaps. His shirt was unbuttoned at the throat and he was leaning forward, his hands clasped between his knees as if he happened to be sitting there in the sun when someone came along and snapped his picture. Someone he liked must have been holding the camera, because he was smiling.

Ashamed of herself for looking into someone else's wallet, Jean snapped it shut, returned to her seat, and gathered up the property she was guarding. She continued to watch the rehearsal, but her thoughts persisted in returning to that snapshot somewhere in the heap on her lap. It seemed to her that knowing a boy well enough to carry his picture in her wallet must be one of the happiest experiences a girl could have.

On the stage Johnny read from his script. "And now time dances on! Allemand right and dos-a-dos—" There was a suggestion of a square-dance caller's sing-song in his voice. On the next-to-the-last word Homer closed his book and picked up his violin. On the last word he began to play *Turkey in the Straw,* with the other violinists. The curtain parted on the square dancers.

Johnny Chessler, thought Jean, I elect you the Boy Whose Snapshot I Would Most Like to Carry in My Wallet.

As the show took shape Jean had more to do. No longer a mere holder of wallets, she helped take inventory of the costumes in the storeroom behind the auditorium, to see what the school had on hand that could be used for the show. When the Costume Club decided it could make the costumes for the Indian maidens, she stayed after school to stitch the brown outing-flannel dresses and to snip the lower edges into fringe. She also helped make up the list of costumes to be rented, including a suit of evening clothes for the narrator. She could hardly wait for the dress rehearsal.

The day the costume rental company's truck backed up to the side door of the auditorium was an exciting one. As the workmen carried racks of costumes into the building, the room backstage became crowded with crinolines, pantalets, Indian headdresses, bat wings, white wigs, parasols, several horse costumes, and parts and pieces of costumes that Jean did not recognize. There was one costume she looked for and did not find—the costume for Johnny. "Where are the evening clothes for the narrator?" she asked Mitsuko, as the two girls were pressing ruffles on some Gay Nineties dresses at the ironing boards in the sewing room. "It was on the list, and I didn't find it any-place."

"Mr. Kohler crossed it off," answered Mitsuko. "He decided Johnny didn't need to appear. That would save the rental of one costume, and it would be more effective if the audience just heard his voice. The disembodied voice of time marching on, I guess."

That was a disappointment, but one which Jean did

not have time to dwell on. Because she was not a particularly skillful seamstress capable of fitting coats and
bodices, Jean was assigned the job of handing out costumes to members of the cast. This was a task which
Jean enjoyed. She stood behind the Dutch door, and as
members of the cast requested their costumes, she located on the racks whatever it was they were to wear.
Touching the various fabrics was a pleasure, and it
was interesting to see how inexpensive materials had
been used to achieve the greatest effect. Jean had
handed out a Civil War uniform (Confederate—tall)
across the Dutch door, when Johnny looked in to see
what was going on. Maybe this was her moment to ask
him.

Peggy Jo appeared behind him, and Johnny stepped
aside. "Blue dress with hoop skirt," said Peggy Jo.

"Blue dress with hoop skirt coming up," answered
Jean, glad of the opportunity to disappear behind a
rack of costumes to try to calm herself. She had to ask
him, and he had to say yes. Now—as soon as Peggy Jo
leaves. Johnny, will you go to the Girls' Association
Dance with me? She had the words lined up on the tip
of her tongue, ready to be spoken.

While Jean slipped the blue dress from its hanger, a
chorus of war whoops came from the Dutch door.
Well, thought Jean, that takes care of that. A girl
could not ask a boy to go to a dance with her when a
bunch of Indians were whooping over his shoulder.
When Jean carried Peggy Jo's costume to the Dutch
door, Johnny was gone. Feeling let down, Jean set
about gathering up an armload of war bonnets. Surely
the next time she saw him . . .

Elaine, who was wearing her outing-flannel dress
and had a turkey feather stuck in a band around her
head, elbowed her way through the group of Indians,
clasped her hands, and sang, " 'For I'll be calling
you—oo—oo—oo.' "

Jean wished Elaine was not so anxious to call attention to herself. The boys would only laugh at her.

"Let's scalp her," suggested one of the Indians.

"There isn't time," said Jean, smiling at the Indians as she shoved their costumes across the Dutch door. Smiling at boys, now that she was taking part in a school activity, was getting easier every day. "Go try on your costumes."

Elaine lingered by the door while half a dozen girls who were to be bats came to collect their chartreuse leotards and black wings.

Jean consulted a list. "Your fingernails haven't come yet," she told the bats, "but the rest of your costumes are ready to try on."

"What fingernails?" asked the bats.

"The bats all wear glittery fingernails eight inches long," answered Jean.

The bats were entranced with the thought of eight-inch fingernails.

"Did you ask him?" whispered Elaine as soon as the bats had trooped off to the dressing room.

Jean pretended to find something wrong with a beard that one of the boys was to wear in the Rip Van Winkle skit. She was beginning to be annoyed by Elaine's intense interest. She was so—so pushy where boys were concerned. You would almost think she was the one who was going to ask Johnny.

"Well, did you?" insisted Elaine. "I saw you talking to him."

"No, Elaine," said Jean. "I haven't."

Elaine must have sensed the change in Jean's feeling toward her, because she sounded crestfallen when she spoke. "Oh. I just wondered, is all."

"There were so many people around." Jean did not want to hurt Elaine's feelings. "Don't you think the bats will look spooky with their long fingernails? I think the haunted-house number will be one of the best in the show."

"Yes," said Elaine, whose feelings had been hurt. "Yes, I guess it will."

Gradually the show took shape. Scenery was painted, the orchestra rehearsed, lines memorized, dances perfected, songs sung. After Jean checked out the costumes for fitting, she checked them in again. While various parts of the show rehearsed in the gymnasium or the band room or wherever they could find space to work in, Jean assisted with several of the simpler alterations. She basted up the hems of some dresses worn by square dancers and sewed an artificial rose on the hip of a dress from the 1920's, to be worn in the Charleston number.

And then came the afternoon of dress rehearsal, the day that Jean would surely ask Johnny to go to the dance. She had to ask him. She was tired of waiting for exactly the right moment, weary of carrying the question on the tip of her tongue. The worst he could do was to say no, and if that was the way it was to be, she wanted to find out now. She did not want this awful suspense to spoil her fun the night of the actual performance.

The minute school was out, Jean rushed to the costume room to start handing out the costumes. This time, because the cast was going to run through the entire show, from beginning to end, it was important that everyone be dressed on time. Out in the auditorium the orchestra was tuning up. Backstage there was the sound of hammering and the shout of "Heads!" that always preceded the lowering of a piece of scenery. Johnny, may I take you to the Girls' Association Dance? Once more Jean lined up the words on her tongue as she handed costumes across the Dutch door. Johnny, will you go to the Girls' Association Dance with me? Outside in the auditorium Mr. Kohler shouted, "Will the singers *please* stand under the *microphones*?"

Mrs. Rankin, adviser of the Costume Club, pushed open the lower half of the Dutch door and entered the room. "All right, girls, let's try to issue the costumes a little faster," she said briskly. "We can't waste time this afternoon. Jean, I'm putting you in charge of the bats' fingernails. Take this box to the dressing room and give each bat ten fingernails, and after rehearsal see that you collect ten fingernails from each girl."

"Yes, Mrs. Rankin." Jean certainly wouldn't have a chance to see Johnny in the girls' dressing room. That question on the tip of her tongue seemed to grow heavier by the minute.

On her way to the dressing room she caught a glimpse of Johnny, surrounded by a group of admiring girls. Jean's acrobatic heart managed to leap because she was looking at Johnny and at the same time to sink because there were so many girls with him. This was not the moment. Scurrying down the hall with her box of fingernails, she found consolation in the thought that there was safety in numbers. All those girls couldn't be asking Johnny to go to the dance. Not at the same time.

The dressing room was a whirl of activity. Girls in their slips waited for members of the club to help them with their hoop skirts. Indian maidens ran around in their bare feet. Girls in the long-waisted, short-skirted dresses of the 1920's, knees close together, stood in front of the mirrors, kicked up their heels in the steps of the Charleston, and collapsed on the benches in fits of giggles. The bats, all twenty of them, were wearing their chartreuse leotards with black bands crisscrossed from waist to shoulder, and helping one another fasten on their black wings.

"Anyone ready for fingernails?" asked Jean, opening her box.

"Oh, look!" cried the bats, as they clustered around Jean.

Jean began to hand out the sparkle-encrusted plastic fingernails to the bats, who slipped them over their fingertips and held out their hands for admiration. "Aren't we glamorous?" they crowed, twinkling their fingertips for everyone to see. Girls in less exotic costumes crowded around to admire.

"You look positively Fu Manchu," said Elaine.

"Lo, the poor Indian in her brown-flannel nightgown," answered a bat, as she flitted over to the mirror to admire herself.

Mrs. Rankin bustled into the dressing room with an armload of white wigs. "All right, minuet girls. Here are your wigs. We have to return them in good condition, so it is not necessary to let the entire student body try them on. We are not going to take time for full make-up today. Three of each group report to the make-up room, so we can get the effect. Jean, if all the bats have their fingernails, see if you can't help some of the other girls."

Jean, who had hoped to escape from the dressing room to someplace backstage where she might see Johnny, looked around for someone to help.

"I need help, Mrs. Rankin," said Peggy Jo. "The hem is coming out of my skirt and I am afraid I wil trip on it."

"There is your chance, Jean," directed Mrs. Ranki "Are all the jitterbug girls wearing saddle shoes ai white socks? We don't want any ballerina slippers this number."

With needle and thread Jean went to the assista of Peggy Jo, who had accidentally caught her foo the hem of her sweeping skirt of the 1860's. Outsic the auditorium Mr. Kohler called out, "Don't fi we are timing this show!" Jean knelt and qu basted up the hem of Peggy Jo's blue brocaded

When she stood up she paused to admire the tall girl in the dress with the drop shoulders. "You look lovely," Jean said truthfully. Even with her blond hair skinned back in an untidy knot, Peggy Jo was beautiful.

"Thank you," said Peggy Jo, her eyes on the mirror.

Jean studied her a moment. "Maybe I shouldn't suggest it," she said shyly, "but I think your hair would look awfully pretty with that dress if you wore it down instead of pinned up."

"Oh, yes, Peggy Jo," said Mitsuko enthusiastically, as she tied a sash for one of the square dancers. "Please take down your hair."

"All right." Peggy Jo quickly pulled the pins out of the knot, so that her fair straight hair tumbled over her shoulders.

"Look!" cried a Charleston girl. "Peggy Jo has taken her hair down."

"Isn't it beautiful?" asked Jean admiringly.

"But I can't wear it this way," protested Peggy Jo, studying herself in the mirror.

"Give me your comb," said Jean. "Maybe I can fix it."

Peggy Jo dug her comb out of her purse and handed it to Jean.

"I think she should wear it hanging straight down her back," said one of the girls.

"With a flower over one ear," added another.

Jean combed back the hair so that it hung straight and heavy. It must be wonderful to have such beautiful hair, so thick and soft to touch.

Mitsuko produced a pink camellia, which she said she had snitched from a bush outside the auditorium (the gardener shouldn't mind this once, because it was for art, wasn't it?) and helped Jean secure it behind Peggy Jo's ear with bobby pins.

"Perfect!" exclaimed the girls, and Jean agreed.

Peggy Jo smiled at herself in the mirror and said nothing.

"Everyone out front," cried Mrs. Rankin. "Now as soon as your number is over, come backstage, change your clothes, turn in your costumes, and *quietly* return to the auditorium by the side door. Minuet girls, be careful of those wigs. Bats, don't tear your wings, and be sure you turn in your fingernails to Jean Jarrett after your act. We don't want any nine-fingered bats during tomorrow night's performance. Now hurry along."

The cast and the members of the Costume Club crowded out of the dressing room, through the backstage area, and down the steps at the front of the stage. Jean saw Johnny standing by a microphone in the wings.

"Hey!" exclaimed Johnny, when he saw the bats. "You can haunt my house any time."

"Hi, Johnny," said Peggy Jo.

Johnny whistled.

"All that and a Chevrolet, too," remarked a stagehand.

Jean, carried along by the crowd, felt a twinge of some uncomfortable emotion. It wasn't envy and it wasn't jealousy. It was more a feeling of dissatisfaction with herself, a foolish feeling because she neither expected nor wanted to be the kind of girl boys whistled at. And she was bothered by something else. Maybe some people did make fun of feminine intuition, but Jean knew—as certainly as she was wearing white saddle shoes—from the way Peggy Jo looked at Johnny, that Peggy Jo liked Johnny and liked him a lot. And I helped make her even more beautiful than she usually is, thought Jean.

"Hi, Jean," Johnny called, as she descended the steps into the auditorium.

Jean smiled radiantly. "Guess what I am," she called

gaily. "Vice-president in charge of bats' fingernails!" It was good to know she was not completely over-shadowed by Peggy Jo.

"Hi, Jean."

Jean looked around and located Homer, his violin resting on his knee, sitting in the orchestra pit.

"Oh—hi, Homer," she answered, thinking that he must have just had his crinkly hair cut. Or perhaps *mowed* was a better word.

"House lights!" bellowed Mr. Kohler. The auditorium grew dim. The orchestra played a medley of music used in the show, and then the voice of the invisible Johnny filled the auditorium.

> "Welcome one and all!
> Come with us year by year
> From then to now, from there to here,
> In song and dance and skit.
> We hope our show will make a hit."

Jean's admiration was wholehearted. Johnny was every bit as good as any announcer she had heard on radio or television. The curtains parted on the Indian scene, and after noticing with amusement Elaine standing on an artificial rock in her brown outing-flannel Indian dress, Jean drifted off in a daydream in which Johnny was saying, and she was replying, Why, yes, Jean, I'd like to go to the Girls' Association Dance with you and don't worry about trasportation. I can get the car. Oh, Johnny, that will be wonderful! That's all right, Jean. I am looking forward to going to the dance with you.

If only it would happen that way.

It seemed to Jean that the show had scarcely begun when the bats were leaping and twirling eerily through the moss-hung trees. She pulled herself out of her daydream long enough to admire the effectiveness of the glittering fingernails, which were her responsibility. And then it was time to slip through the side door and around to the dressing room.

The bats, breathless from dancing, came crowding into the dressing room and flung themselves down on the benches. "How did we look from out front?" someone asked Jean.

"Eerie. Just the way you should look," answered Jean, holding out her box. "Fingernails, please."

"I think we should wear black leotards," said another girl. "Whoever heard of a chartreuse bat?"

"Maybe you are right," agreed another girl. "Don't you think so, Jean?"

"What?" asked Jean, who had been thinking about Johnny.

"Don't you think black leotards would look better?" repeated the girl.

Jean was flattered to have her opinion asked. "No," she said, after considering the matter. "All-black costumes in the dim light would not be nearly as effective. Fingernails, please."

"I guess you are right," mused the bat.

Plainly the bats were in no hurry to part with their fingernails. "Fingernails, *please*," said Jean.

"Can't we wear them awhile?" pleaded a bat, twinkling her fingers. "I have always wanted to have really long fingernails, but my mother won't let me. She's so mid-Victorian about things like that."

"No," said Jean, feeling desperation growing within her.

Girls from other acts were coming in to change their costumes, and the dressing room was once more a scene of confusion. Each girl wanted to discuss her part with anyone who would listen. Jean looked into her box. She had collected fingernails from not more than half a dozen bats.

Jean made a decision. If she was ever going to ask

Johnny to go to the dance, she had to do it now. That very minute. She set her box on a bench, stepped up on the bench, clapped her hands, and as the voices subsided and she had attention for an instant, she announced resolutely, "All bats will deposit their fingernails in this box at once. Mrs. Rankin's orders."

I am not acting like me at all, Jean marveled, as she hopped off the bench and pushed her way out of the dressing room. That was the thing to do, she decided—go right on not acting like herself. Be somebody else for a change. She ran down the hall and up the steps to the area backstage. She heard the cowboys singing and caught a glimpse of their campfire, red electric bulbs under crumpled paper this time, instead of a wastebasket, and saw their horses standing in the background. A ripple of laughter went through the audience as the horses stepped out of the shadows and began to dance. But Johnny—where was Johnny?

"Only members of the stage crew are supposed to be backstage," someone reminded Jean.

Jean paid no attention. She had to find Johnny. Now. She tripped over a prop and as she bent to rub her leg, she saw Johnny leaning against the wall in the wings toward the front of the stage, waiting for his cue. While she made her way around the artificial rocks that had been removed from the stage after the Indian number, the cowboys and horses finished their act and after the curtain had been drawn, trooped into the wings.

Jean got around the last rock, stood in front of Johnny, looked him straight in the eye, and in her determination spoke almost belligerently. "Johnny, will you go to the Girls' Association Dance with me?" This was not the way she had meant to sound at all, but at least her tongue was free of the weight of those words she had carried about with her all through rehearsals.

"Narrator!" bellowed Mr. Kohler, from the rear of the auditorium. "We are wasting time! Where is our narrator?"

Johnny grinned at Jean and tweaked a lock of her hair before he answered, "Sure, Jean. I'll go with you." Then he turned on the microphone and filled the auditorium with his voice.

Jean stood where she was, stunned and elated by her good fortune. Johnny had accepted! He really had. Johnny Chessler was going to the dance with Jean Jarrett. *Johnny Chessler*. She could hardly wait to tell the news to Sue.

Then, because Jean was conscientious, she turned and climbed around the rocks once more and ran on light feet back to the dressing room to count the bats' fingernails.

CHAPTER
7

The days following the variety show were happy ones for Jean. Sue, who had said with good grace, "All right, I'm wrong," when she heard that Johnny had accepted Jean's invitation, had another date with Kenneth Cory and had decided that she could, if she really put her mind to it, slip-cover her father's chair, which was really terribly shabby. Jean, thinking how the house would look when Johnny came to see her, said that Sue was absolutely right: that chair was a disgrace. Mrs. Jarrett suggested that it might be easier to upholster than to slip-cover, because the old cover could be used for a pattern. Sue agreed, and after Mrs. Jarrett had found a good buy at Fabrics, Etc., the two girls and their mother fell to work on the chair. Mr. Jarrett muttered good-naturedly that a man couldn't even call his favorite chair his own when he lived in a houseful of women, but as long as he wouldn't have any place to sit for a few days he had better do something about the cracks in the plaster over the door into the hall, and while he was at it he might as well give the living room and dining room a coat of paint.

Because Jean actually had a date with Johnny now, she felt free to join him and his friends during lunch hour. Johnny continued to meet her outside the sewing room after school and to walk out of the building with her. That week Jean felt she had only one problem, but that problem, unfortunately, was serious. She had no transportation for the dance.

It was not until Thursday evening that Jean found courage to broach the subject to her father. She did not often find her father alone, but this evening Sue, who had done her homework after school, was in the bedroom stitching on the new upholstery. Mrs. Jarrett was in the breakfast nook going through the advertisements in the evening paper and making a list of bargains to be the basis of her weekly shopping list. Mr. Jarrett was in the living room painting the walls with a roller. It seemed like a perfect opportunity.

"By the way, Daddy," began Jean, perching on the arm of a chair covered with an old sheet. "Maybe you have heard me mention it already, but Johnny is going to the Girls' Association Dance with me . . . and I wondered if you would mind driving us in the car."

Mr. Jarrett dipped the roller into a tray of paint and rolled it back and forth. "Jean," he said, keeping his voice low, "I want to have a little talk with you."

"Yes, Daddy," answered Jean in a whisper, as her hopes wilted. Her parents so rarely found it necessary to have little talks with their daughters that her father's words sounded ominous. Without transportation she could hardly take Johnny to the dance.

"Jean, I don't want you running after this fellow, Johnny," said Mr. Jarrett, running the roller over the wall above the mantel.

"Daddy, the girls are *supposed* to ask the boys to go to this dance." Jean glanced apprehensively at her father, who was too busy watching his work to look at her. Didn't he understand these things? "The boys can't ask the girls this time."

"I haven't noticed Johnny taking you anyplace," said Mr. Jarrett.

"I see him every day after school," said Jean, "and he came over one Saturday and took me out for a Coke. I told you about that. And last Friday was the variety show, so he couldn't make a date that night. And it wasn't his fault he couldn't come over that time he was supposed to. His father . . ." Jean's arguments diminished into silence. Nervously she twisted her fingers.

"Would you rather have braised short ribs or shoulder lamb chops?" Mrs. Jarrett asked from the breakfast nook. "They are both on special this weekend."

When neither Jean nor her father answered, Sue called from the bedroom, "Let's have shoulder lamb chops. Braised short ribs are just stew meat with bones. And don't forget to put soap powder on the list. We are just about out."

"Anything else you can think of?" asked Mrs. Jarrett.

"Isn't some market having a special on asparagus?" asked Sue.

"I'll see," replied Mrs. Jarrett. "Asparagus would taste good for a change."

Shoulder lamb chops and soap powder, at what was practically the most important moment in her whole life! Jean searched her father's face for some sign that he might give her an affirmative answer to her question. It would be so much easier if they lived in a house big enough for two conversations at the same time. . . .

"I'm not going to have my girls running after boys," said Mr. Jarrett. "Let the boys run after you."

Jean stifled an impatient sigh and forgot to whisper. "Daddy, I'm *not*. Just tell me, will you drive us to the dance?"

"How late does this dance last?" asked Jean's father.

And now they had to go into that. "Midnight," answered Jean.

"Midnight!" It was easy to see that Mr. Jarrett did not approve.

"Daddy, it is Saturday night," pleaded Jean. "It isn't as though it was a school night or you had to go to work the next morning."

"It seems to me that midnight is pretty late for a fifteen-year-old girl to be out," said Mr. Jarrett.

"Not on Saturday." Jean did not want to argue with her father but she could not avoid it. She wanted a promise of transportation, not a discussion of proper hours for fifteen-year-olds. Surely this was not one of those times when her father would be unusually strict, the way he was about baby-sitting.

"Oh, come on, Daddy," Sue called from the bedroom. "Say you'll drive them. It's just this once."

Honestly, the walls in the house were practically tissue paper. Nevertheless, Jean hoped that Sue's word would help.

Mrs. Jarrett came into the living room with her grocery list in her hand. "I'll chauffeur them," she said. "I don't mind."

"Would you, Mother?" asked Jean eagerly, appreciating the offer all the more because Saturday was Mrs. Jarrett's most tiring day at Fabrics, Etc.

"I'll be glad to," said Mrs. Jarrett. "I'm anxious to know what kind of boy Johnny is."

If that wasn't just like a mother, thought Jean. Oh, well, never mind. That was the way mothers were, and there wasn't much a girl could do about it. She finally had a promise of transportation, and that was the important thing.

Mr. Jarrett wiped a speck of paint off the bricks on the front of the fireplace. "All right, but she has to be home by midnight. I know it will mean leaving the dance early, but midnight is plenty late enough for a girl her age." He still did not look as though he approved.

There are times when it is best for a girl to give in gracefully, and this was one of them. "All right, Daddy," agreed Jean. She had a date, she had transportation. Let the problem of leaving early enough take care of itself when the time came. "I'll be Cinderella, but I won't leave my slipper behind, because we can't afford to scatter shoes around."

Jean felt so lighthearted that she skipped down the street like a little girl on her way to Elaine's house, where she was going to study and keep Elaine company, because the Mundys were going out for the evening. After Jean told Elaine her good news, the girls settled down with their books at the kitchen table.

It was not long before Elaine looked up from her Spanish book. "What a silly sentence. 'Mary is carrying her cat in a basket.' Any cat I know would jump out before she had gone two feet. It isn't a basket with a lid, either, because there is a picture. By the way— have you forgotten about Saturday afternoon?" she asked.

Saturday afternoon? "What about Saturday afternoon?" asked Jean, unable to recall what it was she was supposed to remember.

"Kip Laddish's personal appearance," said Elaine.

"Oh—Elaine." Jean was genuinely contrite. "I completely forgot. I am terribly sorry." It seemed to her that Kip Laddish had gone out of her life a long, long time ago. It had been weeks since she had even remembered to watch his program.

Elaine looked speculatively at her friend. "Tell me something," she said slowly. "You don't really want to go, do you?"

Jean hesitated. She and Elaine knew one another too well not to be honest, but at the same time, she did not want to hurt Elaine's feelings. Her hesitation was answer enough.

Elaine's usual exuberance faded. "You don't want to go. I can tell."

"Elaine . . ." Jean began, and found she did not know what to say. Going to the personal appearance of a singer who made popular records now seemed like such a childish thing to do that she felt ashamed that she had ever wanted to go in the first place. Why, they had even planned to try to get his autograph—it embarrassed her to even think of that now. However, she did not want to disappoint Elaine, who had given her on Christmas morning an envelope containing a hand-printed certificate saying that Elaine Mundy promised to give Jean Jarrett one (1) paid admission to the personal appearance of Kip Laddish.

"I know how it is." Elaine smiled ruefully. "Things are different when you have a real boy to think about. Not that Kip is unreal, exactly, but for us he might as well be somebody we imagined."

"I'll go with you, Elaine," said Jean. "I just forgot, is all."

Elaine shook her head. "It wouldn't be the same now that you have Johnny."

Jean could not deny the truth of this. And she was glad she no longer wanted to stand in line with a lot of giggling girls to see a singer who needed a haircut.

It seemed a silly waste of time and money. Why, I have gone through a stage, thought Jean triumphantly. I must be growing up.

Elaine, who was never disheartened long, seemed to perk up. "Now the trouble is, I owe you a Christmas present."

"Oh, Elaine," Jean laughed. "That's all right. It's enough that you wanted to take me."

"No," said Elaine seriously. "I'll think of something to take the place of a ticket for the personal appearance."

"Don't worry about it," said Jean and then, because she wanted to change the subject, asked, "Have you heard from any pen pals lately?"

"A letter from the English girl, Cynthia," replied Elaine. "She wants to know if we have many skyscrapers in Northgate."

Jean giggled. "I wonder if the Pacific Insurance Building counts."

"Or there is the Medical-Dental Building," said Elaine. "That is five stories high, but I don't think either one of them exactly scrapes the sky. Cynthia also wants me to describe an American drugstore. She has heard they sell everything and she wants to know if they really do."

"You could tell her that the Low Cost sells Easter bunnies, garden hose, and split-leaf philodendron. That ought to answer her question," said Jean, thinking that she had been too busy sewing on stoles and dreaming about Johnny to write letters. "I haven't heard from any of my pen pals lately."

"I wonder if they have Easter bunnies in England," remarked Elaine. "Cynthia also sent a snapshot of herself. She was standing in what looked like a park, holding her hand out to a deer."

Snapshot—Johnny, ran Jean's thoughts, because any subject could remind her of Johnny. Johnny, the Boy

Whose Snapshot I Would Most Like to Carry in My Wallet.

"I guess I should send her a snapshot of me, but I don't have any recent ones," said Elaine, "except that one Dad took of me wearing my shorts at the mountains last summer and I look like Ichabod Crane or something. Oh, well. Don't forget we are supposed to be studying."

Jean bent her head over her books, but an idea was stirring in the back of her mind.

"Ah, this is better," remarked Elaine, and began to translate, " 'Here comes John's dog. The cat jumps out of the basket. Run, run, cat.' I knew that cat wouldn't stay in a basket."

"Elaine, if we had a camera I could take your picture," suggested Jean. The idea was taking definite shape. "Cynthia might like a picture of you taken at school." The idea was now ready to hatch. "Lots of people take cameras to school in good weather, and I could take your picture during lunch hour when everybody is outside milling around. And then—maybe we could sort of casually snap Johnny's picture. I mean— if you wouldn't mind. I would love to have his snapshot and I would pay for the film developing out of my stole money."

"And then you could carry his picture in your wallet." Elaine took it from there. "And leave your wallet open accidentally on purpose so everybody could see that you are carrying Johnny's picture in it!"

"Well, not exactly," said Jean. "Everybody knows that I don't really know Johnny that well. But I would like to have his picture to keep in my corner of the mirror." For some inexplicable reason Jean felt that owning a snapshot of Johnny would help her to feel more sure of him.

"You don't have to pay for anything. The picture will be my Christmas present to you," said Elaine enthusiastically. "I'll take Dad's good camera, if he will let me, and we'll take a good picture."

Since the girls were supposed to be studying, the implications of this remark did not strike Jean until the next morning, when she stopped for Elaine on the way to school. Elaine came to the door with a camera in a brown case slung over one shoulder. Over the other shoulder she carried a tripod. "I have the light meter in my pocket," she said.

"Oh, Elaine, not the tripod," protested Jean. "Nobody takes a tripod to school."

"We want to take a good picture," Elaine pointed out. "This is your Christmas present."

That was the trouble with Elaine. Her co-operation was too wholehearted. "But I don't want Johnny to think we planned to take his picture," Jean explained. "It wouldn't look casual if we have to set up a tripod and everything. I would rather snap his pictire quickly when he wasn't even looking."

"Well—all right." Regretfully Elaine left the tripod behind. "He usually hangs around that urn by the front steps after he eats his lunch. Maybe we could catch him then."

Jean agreed that this would be a good time to take Johnny's picture. "Maybe it would be better if you took the picture," she suggested as they started toward school. "Then he could think—if he noticed you, that is—that you were just taking a picture of a bunch of kids on the steps of the school. You know. Like those snapshots they publish in the back of the yearbook."

"That's a good idea," agreed Elaine. "That way maybe you could be in the picture too. You could walk over and ask him something, and I could creep up and snap the picture without his knowing it."

"I think that might work." A snapshot of herself and Johnny, to be able to see the two of them in black and white—this would be even better than having one of Johnny alone. And maybe if—no, not if, *when*—she got to know Johnny better she could tell him about the snapshot. And maybe he would remark, Say, I'd like to have a copy to carry in my wallet. And she would say, "I'll have a copy made for you, Johnny. And he would say eagerly, Would you? I'd sure like to have a picture of us together.

At noon Jean and Elaine hurried through their lunch, which to Jean was tasteless. Her thoughts were not on food that day. Then they went to the "Girls," where they combed their hair and carefully refreshed their lipstick. "Let's hurry and take your picture before Johnny and his gang get there," said Jean anxiously. "Do I look all right?"

"You look fine," answered Elaine. "Now remember, just be casual when you walk over to Johnny. Don't jitter or he will suspect something is up."

But when Jean and Elaine reached the front steps of Northgate High, they found that Johnny and some of his friends were already there. "Hi, Johnny," said Jean, and whispered to Elaine, "I'll go ahead and take your picture first, the way we planned."

Elaine removed the camera from its case and handed it to Jean. "You look in here and press here," she instructed Jean before she leaned against the geranium-filled urn at one side of the steps and smiled fixedly into the camera.

"Smile at the birdie," Johnny called across the steps. Knowing that Johnny was watching made Jean's hands tremble as she peered into the finder.

"Come closer," said Elaine. "For outdoor close-ups you are supposed to be five feet away from your subject."

Still looking into the finder, Jean moved closer and tripped on the steps.

"Hey, look out!" cautioned Elaine. "That's Dad's good camera."

"Sorry." Jean was ashamed that Johnny had seen her being so clumsy. She managed to center Elaine in the jiggling finder and to snap the picture.

"I just know I had my eyes closed." Elaine's voice was a shade too loud, as if she was eager to call attention to herself.

"I'll take another," offered Jean, hoping that Johnny would lose interest and turn his attention elsewhere.

"Maybe you better," agreed Elaine. This time she sat on the steps, crossed her ankles, and gazed off into the distance.

Some of the boys with Johnny whistled. "A regular pin-up girl," one of them said, and the others laughed.

Still self-conscious because Johnny was watching, Jean once more centered her friend in the finder that refused to stand still, and pressed the button. "That should be a good one," she said, not because she thought it could be a clear picture when her hands had been trembling, but because she wanted to say something that would make her appear at ease in Johnny's eyes.

"The light meter," said Elaine as she took the camera from Jean. "We forgot to use the light meter."

"Does it really matter?" asked Jean, not anxious to take Elaine's picture a third time.

"I don't know," admitted Elaine, "but Dad always uses it." Then she said under her breath, "Go over near Johnny and act nonchalant."

"Elaine, I *can't*," whispered Jean, losing her courage. "He will guess what we are up to."

"No, he won't. I'll do it so he will never guess. Now go on." After this assurance Elaine said, in a clear, firm voice, "Well, I guess I'll take some snapshots around school. If they are any good maybe the yearbook can use them."

Jean did not move.

"Go *on*," whispered Elaine.

Reluctantly Jean started toward Johnny. In a way, it must be nice to be like Elaine, who was never bashful, instead of always feeling too shy to do the things she wanted to do. "Hello, Johnny," said Jean. "I just wanted to tell you it is all right about transportation for the dance. Mother said she would drive uts."

"That's good." Johnny grinned down at Jean.

"I just thought I would tell you," said Jean. She enjoyed standing beside Johnny—after all, she did have a date with him. Out of the corner of her eye she could see Elaine focusing the camera. Jean, who could not think of a thing to say to Johnny, felt her smile grow strained. She glimpsed Elaine holding up the light meter. Hurry, Elaine, Jean thought desperately. Never mind the light meter. Just take the picture any old way.

"Hey, Elaine!" It was Homer who called out from beside a pillar at the top of the steps. "You girls forgot to wind the film."

Elaine groaned and the crowd laughed. Wouldn't you know, thought Jean.

It seemed to Jean that the crowd grew every minute. And Johnny would probably guess that the reason she had forgotten to turn the film was that she was flustered because he was watching. At the same time the thought flashed through her mind that Homer must have been standing there taking in the whole performance.

Elaine wound the film and looked into the finder once more.

Jean, suffering because this snapshot had taken too long and attracted too much attention, found herself, like an animal caught in the glare of headlights, unable to move. Snap it, Elaine, she thought. Snap it and get it over with before Johnny guesses what we are doing.

"Elaine, you will have better light if you move out of that shadow," Homer called from the top of the steps.

Homer, you keep out of this, Jean thought fiercely, as Elaine did as she was told. At least, Johnny seemed unconcerned about it all. It was just possible that he still thought Elaine was taking a picture of the front of the school. Still facing Johnny, Jean turned her eyes toward Elaine to see what was keeping her from taking the picture this time.

At that moment Elaine pressed the button. Jean quickly looked up to see if Johnny had noticed, and found that Johnny was smiling directly into the lens of the camera. He had not only noticed, he had posed. Jean's feelings were in a state of confusion. The snapshot should be a good one—of Johnny, at least—if Elaine had the right distance and had made the right adjustments, but Johnny must have guessed what they were doing. She wondered what he thought.

"This time I'll remember to turn the film," Elaine remarked to the crowd, but by this time only Jean was interested.

"Let's go around to the playing field," suggested Johnny, to the group around him. "Some of the track team is practicing."

"Good idea," agreed someone, and the group started to move from the steps.

Does Johnny mean me, too, Jean wondered.

"Coming, Jean?" asked Johnny, as the others started to go around the building.

"Yes," answered Jean happily. She glanced back at Elaine, whose eyes were saying so plainly, Include me. Please include me.

Johnny put his hand casually on Jean's shoulder, but Jean's instant pleasure was spoiled by the longing look on Elaine's face. Poor Elaine, standing there with the camera in her hands and one side of her hem sagging. It should have been so easy to say, You come, too, Elaine, but somehow Jean could not make the words come out. She felt too insecure with Johnny and his friends to include Elaine. As she walked along with Johnny she tried to catch Elaine's eye, to receive a glance that would show that Elaine understood her feelings.

But Elaine was busy fitting the camera into its case, the camera that now held the precious impression of Jean and Johnny on its film. It hurt Jean to watch her and she felt ashamed of her own behavior. Elaine looked so forlorn with her hem sagging. Somehow, Jean would have felt better if Elaine's hem had been straight.

CHAPTER
8

With twenty dollars in *a cappella* choir-stole money saved, Jean decided to splurge. Why not? Her first school dance was an important event, a milestone in her life and she wanted to look her best for Johnny. She wanted to read in his face the thought that he had never seen her look so nice before. This time there would be no pattern spread out on the study table, no careful planning to get a dress out of half a yard less material than the pattern called for, no struggles to sew in a zipper. This time Jean would take her twenty dollars, go into a shop, and buy a dress ready-made so that she could be sure ahead of time how she was going to look. It was going to be blissfully luxurious to go forth with money in her pocket, money that was going to buy not only a new dress, but a new adventure as well.

However, Jean was uncertain of her own taste in clothes, timid about going into a dress shop alone. She needed someone to go with her, but who? Elaine? She would like to do something to make up to Elaine for the way she had treated her, but Elaine was the kind of girl who shopped with great enthusiasm and somehow bought all the wrong things. Not that this bothered Elaine, who thought nothing of wearing a plaid coat over a print dress. Her mother? No. Her mother was inclined to be a little old-fashioned in her choice of clothes. Sue? Sue, who had had more experience in sewing, had a good eye for smart lines and becoming colors, but Jean was not sure that she would want to go on this shopping trip, because she was not sure how Sue felt about Johnny. It was always so hard to tell what Sue was thinking. She had managed a graceful show of pleasure when Johnny had accepted Jean's invitation, and she had made no further references to the quarrel about whether he would or would not. Probably her thoughts were so full of Kenneth that she no longer bothered even to think about Johnny.

"Sue?" asked Jean from her end of the study table.

"Hmm?" replied Sue from the other end of the table.

"I want to take my stole money and buy a dress to wear to the dance. A dress-shop dress," said Jean. "Would you come with me?"

"I'd love to," answered Sue, looking up from her books. "Try on lots of dresses, and we will make an afternoon of it. I adore looking at pretty clothes, and it will be lots more fun with money to spend."

Jean knew what Sue meant. Both girls had often visited shops to get ideas for their own sewing, but without money to spend they had always felt like intrud-

ers. They had entered hoping the clerks would all be
so busy that they could look at the dresses on the racks
without assistance. If a clerk did insist on helping,
they managed to invent a reason for leaving. And one
of the nicest parts of this shopping expedition would
be the companionship of a sister who understood.

Saturday turned out to be an exhilarating day,
warm and bright, with an occasional breeze to remind
Jean that this was still spring, that summer had not
come. A beautiful day, and twenty dollars that she had
earned all by herself! Anything could happen. Jean
felt like skipping all the way to the bus stop.

When the girls got off the bus, they wandered along
the main street, pausing in front of windows, uncertain which store to try first. In some shops the windows were full of house dresses, in others the clothing
was too old for a fifteen-year-old girl. "Let's try
Northgate Apparel," said Sue impulsively.

"Isn't that pretty expensive?" Jean was doubtful.
These days twenty dollars, a lot of money to her, did
not seem like much to other people. She knew that
from looking at the fashions in *Vogue*.

"Lots of good shops carry inexpensive dresses," said
Sue. "Anyway, I have always wanted to go in there, so
why not?"

"All right," agreed Jean, who wanted to squeeze every bit of adventure out of her two ten-dollar bills.
"What are we waiting for?"

Together the girls pushed open the heavy glass door
of Northgate Apparel and stepped onto the thick carpet. The shop was cool and filled with soft music that
seemed to come from nowhere. They breathed the dry
fragrance of new clothes.

"Remember," whispered Sue. "Try on lots of
dresses."

"I feel like an impostor," Jean whispered back.

There were few customers in the shop. Several saleswomen, in smart beige or gray dresses with touches of white at the neck, were sitting on chairs at one side of the shop. One of them rose and approached the girls. "Good afternoon," she said. "May I help you?"

"Well . . ." Jean licked her lips. Her resolution to try on lots of dresses wavered. This place was much too elegant for her pocketbook. "Yes . . . I am looking for a—a dress." When the clerk looked as if she did not quite understand, Jean added hastily, "I don't mean a school dress or anything like that." She did not want this woman to think she would come to a shop like Northgate Apparel for a school dress.

"An afternoon dress, perhaps?" queried the clerk.

"Yes, only I'm not going to wear it in the afternoon," said Jean, uncomfortably conscious that her saddle shoes were scuffed under their layer of fresh white cleaner. She wanted an afternoon dress to wear in the evening—that sounded ridiculous, but she could hardly say she wanted an evening dress. That did not sound right, either.

"A dress to wear to a dance," said Sue, taking over. "A school dance."

"I understand," said the clerk. "If you will be seated, I will show you some of the things we have that might be suitable. What size do you wear?"

Jean was not prepared for this question. "Well . . . I take a size twelve pattern, but patterns don't run the same as dresses. And I always have to shorten the patterns," answered Jean, and wished she had not. The clerk did not need to know she was not used to shopping for dresses.

"I think perhaps a nine." The woman looked appraisingly at Jean. "Or even a seven."

When the clerk disappeared, the girls sat down on two gray chairs separated by a table that held copies of *Vogue* and *Harper's Bazaar*. "I hope she does understand," whispered Jean. "Everything looks so expensive." She took comfort in the thought of her slip, a new one that she had been saving since last Christmas for some special occasion.

The saleswoman appeared with several dresses over her arm, one of which she hung on a stand in front of the girls. It was blue linen with embroidered white flowers scattered across the waist. Jean managed to catch a glimpse of the price tag dangling from the sleeve. The dress cost thirty-nine dollars and ninety-five cents. Jean and Sue exchanged a glance that said, Oh, dear, this won't do at all.

"No, I don't think so," said Jean.

The clerk hung a pale yellow dress in front of it. The dangling tag read twenty-nine dollars and ninety-five cents.

"Well . . . no," said Jean, feeling more and more uncomfortable.

Sue was braver. "Don't you have anything for less?" she asked.

"How much did you have in mind?" asked the clerk kindly.

Jean decided she might as well be honest. If the shop did not have anything she could afford, they could leave, couldn't they? It wasn't as though she had no money at all. "I have twenty dollars," she said. Twenty dollars seemed much smaller than it had before they had entered the shop. "I don't suppose you have anything for that."

"Oh, yes. We have lots of dresses at that price. It is the small size that is the problem. Not many people are lucky enough to have a trim little figure like yours." She smiled reassuringly at Jean. "I'll see what I can find."

Jean relaxed. This woman, she felt, really did understand. And it was pleasant to know that she had a trim little figure. She would remember this the next time someone called her Half Pint. A girl wearing a smock appeared and silently removed the dresses the clerk had hung on the stand. "Those dresses are awfully plain to cost so much," whispered Jean.

"Plain things always cost more," Sue whispered back.

The clerk returned with a pink dress, hung it on the rack, looked at Jean, and then critically at the dress. "No," she said definitely. "It won't do at all. Pastels are wrong for you."

Jean, who had thought the dress pretty, looked at the clerk in surprise.

"With your coloring you need unusual colors, odd colors that most people can't wear," said the clerk firmly.

"I do?" Jean had always liked pink and blue. She remembered the dress printed with pink clover that she had admired in a magazine in the library. Was that wrong for her?

The clerk disappeared once more.

"She's right. You aren't the pretty type," said Sue, and then added hastily, as if she feared she might hurt her sister's feelings, "I mean you are not the—the fluffy type."

Jean sighed. "I know what you mean."

The clerk appeared with another batch of dresses over her arm. "I found these in our patio shop," she said, and hung a dress of an unusual shade of green, almost an olive green, on the stand. Jean could see that it was a smart dress, but somehow it was not what she had pictured for herself. "Well . . ." she said doubtfully. "I sort of had a gathered skirt in mind."

"No, not for you," said the clerk definitely. "Little girls are so often overwhelmed by too much skirt." She hung on the stand a pale beige dress of polished cotton with a twisted sash of brown and apricot.

Jean knew that this was her dress. It was not at all the sort of dress she had planned to buy, but she knew at once that it was right for her. "Oh, yes," she said happily. "That is—if it doesn't cost too much."

"It is only seventeen ninety-five," said the clerk, "and it just came in today. We think it has a lot of style for the price."

The girls followed the clerk to the fitting room. "It has to fit," Jean whispered to her sister. When the clerk had left them alone, Jean slipped out of her dress and slid the new dress on over her best slip. When Sue pulled up the zipper for her, Jean faced three views of herself in the mirror. Even though the skirt was too long and her scuffed shoes looked even more shabby, she was completely satisfied with what she saw. "I love it," she said ecstatically, and twirled around for the joy of watching three reflections of the dress in motion. "It is so simple and—"

"Becoming," finished Sue.

"Of course it is too long." Jean knew this was not a real obstacle.

"We can shorten it ourselves," said Sue. "Alterations are terribly expensive."

Jean ran her hands over the polished cotton. "I suppose . . ." she hesitated, not wanting to say the words, but feeling that she should. "I suppose we could make it for a lot less." They could, but it would not be the same.

"We could," agreed Sue, "except I don't think we could find a pattern like it. Or any material exactly that color."

Jean smiled gratefully at her sister because she had answered this argument for not buying the dress.

The clerk swept aside the curtain of the fitting room. "Why don't you come out and look at yourself in the big mirror in the daylight?"

Jean's resolution to try on lots of dresses was completely forgotten. She knew she was going to buy this dress, but she could not resist walking out of the fitting room in it. She was even more delighted with the dress in the daylight. In front of the big mirror Johnny's words, "How's the cute girl?" ran through her thoughts. Now she wondered why she had been surprised to hear him speak the words. She was attractive. She did not need Johnny to tell her. In the reflection she noticed another clerk and a customer glance at her and then pause to look more closely. They, too, recognized that the dress was becoming, that she was an attractive girl.

Jean could find no reason for prolonging this satisfying moment. "I'll take the dress," she said, smiling radiantly at the clerk.

"You have made a wise choice." The clerk returned Jean's smile. "A flared skirt is right for you. You would be lost in a lot of gathers."

I'll remember that, thought Jean gratefully, and I'll remember what she said about color, too.

"And if you don't mind my making a suggestion," continued the clerk, "some linen pumps tinted to match the brown in the sash would set the dress off."

Pumps with heels to make her look taller! If only Jean had enough money.

"I'll lend you the money," said Sue, reading her sister's thoughts.

"Would you?" Jean was touched by her sister's generosity. Since it was settled that she was taking Johnny to the dance, Sue wanted her to look her best and to have a good time.

"I hope you have a wonderful evening," said the clerk, when Jean had taken off the dress and paid for it. "I know there won't be a sweeter-looking girl at the dance."

"Thank you," said Jean, flushing with pleasure as she accepted the box containing the dress that she had earned with her own hands.

The girls left the shop and walked down the street

to Belmonts', the shoe store that advertised free tinting of shoes. They chose a pair of linen pumps that made Jean, who had never worn high heels before, feel as if she were going to pitch forward on her face. When the salesman assured her that the shoes fit correctly, she opened the box from the dress shop and carefully matched the sash to the right shade of brown on the salesman's color card. The shoes would be ready for her to pick up two days later.

"That will give me time to practice walking in heels," Jean told Sue, as they left the shoe store. Then she gave a sigh of pure happiness. A date with Johnny, a pretty new dress, and high heels—all at the same time. And most wonderful of all, now she really believed that she was attractive. The world was brighter, her footsteps lighter. It had been such a happy afternoon that she was reluctant to let it end. "Sue, let's splurge some more," she said impulsively. "I'll treat you to a Coke at Snow's—if you will lend me twenty cents."

Sue laughed. "And recklessly spend two whole dimes?"

"Just fling them to the winds," answered Jean. She and her sister rarely spent money on Cokes. Money, they had learned, could quickly be dribbled away on little things that had no real value.

Having made up their minds, Jean and Sue walked into Snow's, an establishment that was part candy store and part soda fountain. "Mmm. Smell the chocolate," remarked Jean, as she chose a small booth. When the waitress, who wore a starched bow on top of her head, handed her a menu, she read it, because it made such delicious reading, even though she knew she had only a dime to spend. She felt luxurious just reading the prices.

When the waitress had taken Jean's and Sue's orders, two women sat down in a booth that was sepa-

rated from the girls' by a shoulder-high partition.
While the pair settled themselves, Jean noticed that
they were both well dressed and had smart haircuts.
The face of one of the women was unnaturally pink,
as if she might have spent part of the afternoon under a
hair dryer. She wore a neckpiece made of the skins of
several small animals biting one another's tails, which
she pushed back as if she did not enjoy the feel of the
fur against her flushed skin. The other woman wore
an expensively simple black dress, a choker of pearls,
and a flowery hat.

The waitress set two Cokes on small plates covered
with paper doilies and placed two paper-covered
straws in front of Jean and Sue. The girls smiled at
one another across the table. A dress in an elegant box
on the seat beside Jean, Cokes served on paper doilies—so much luxury for one afternoon!

"The *calories*," murmured Fur Neckpiece across the
partition, as she studied the menu.

Once more Jean and Sue exchanged glances, this
time of amusement. Jean felt a little smug, because she
did not have to worry about calories. She had a trim
little figure. The clerk said so. Slowly she pulled the
wrapper from the straw. The cute girl with the trim
little figure was enjoying herself, and she wanted to
make the Cokes last as long as she could.

"Oh, well, I feel reckless," said Flowery Hat. "I'm
going to have a hot fudge sundae and let the calories
fall where they may."

"On me they always fall in the wrong place," answered Fur Neckpiece, "but I think I'll have one too,
and just feel guilty while I eat it."

Jean felt sorry for the two women, who could afford
hot fudge sundaes but could not wholeheartedly enjoy
them. Poor things. It must be dreadful to be middle-
aged, able to afford those nice fattening sweets, and

have to worry about calories. How much nicer to be
fifteen and have a trim little figure!

"Tell me," said Flowery Hat, "how is that handsome
son of yours?"

Fur Neckpiece laughed lightly. "He's still the same
old charmer."

"Madly pursued by all the girls?" asked Flowery
Hat.

"Oh, my, yes," answered Fur Neckpiece, in mock
weariness. "And by one girl in particular. Poor little
thing."

"Doesn't he like her?" Flowery Hat asked.

Fur Neckpiece poured hot fudge from a pitcher over
her ice cream. "I suppose he is flattered. After all,
what boy wouldn't be? It is really too funny for words.
She has a friend, and the two of them walk past our
house, although I am sure they live nowhere near—
probably they hope to run into him—and they giggle."

Jean let her straw stand in her Coke. She knew with
a terrible certainty who the girl was they were talking
about. Jean Jarrett was being gossiped about over two
hot fudge sundaes. If only Sue were not there to listen,
too.

"And she invents excuses to telephone," Fur Neckpiece continued. "When I was a girl I wouldn't have
dreamed of telephoning a boy. I didn't have to. They
telephoned me."

"What is the girl like?" asked Flowery Hat.

"Oh, just a girl—no one you would ever notice," answered Fur Neckpiece.

Jean had no appetite for her Coke. This could not
be Johnny's mother, because things like this did not
happen, but who else could she be? Everything she
said fitted like—like that shoe everybody said you
should wear if it fits. This shoe was custom-made.

"She even asked him to go to a school dance," Fur
Piece went on.

Jean lifted her eyes to Sue, who was looking at the doily under her Coke while she sipped through her straw. Sue's face was grave.

"Of course the dance is girl's choice, but she asked him so far ahead he had to say yes." Fur Piece poured more hot fudge over her ice cream and scraped out the pitcher with her spoon.

"I think your new dress is terribly becoming," said Sue, in a clear voice, because she did not want to give the two women the impression that she and Jean were eavesdropping.

"Yes, isn't it?" Jean managed to say, and missed part of the conversation in the next booth. Once more Jean looked at Sue, whose face was filled with concern. If Sue is going to start being sympathetic, I can't bear it, Jean thought. I simply can't bear it.

"He's really a very good-natured boy," the mother of the charmer was saying. "But he was hoping another girl would ask him. Of course, there wasn't much he could do, when this girl asked him so far in advance."

Was two weeks too far ahead? Surely not, but Jean was not certain, because she had never asked a boy to go to a dance before. Jean longed to look more closely at the boy's mother, but she did not dare turn her head. And then the wild thought crossed her mind that perhaps the woman had recognized her as the girl who walked past Johnny's house and giggled. Perhaps she was saying all this for her particular benefit.

Jean longed to say to Sue, Come on, let's leave, but her tongue felt too stiff to speak, her feet too heavy to walk. When she picked up her Coke, her hands shook so that the ice rattled in the glass, and she had to set it down again. And there was Sue, beginning to look sympathetic. Jean longed to melt and disappear with her ice. Her world had been reduced to ravelings.

"Poor Roger," remarked Flowery Hat. "He will always be pursued by girls."

Roger. The boy they were talking about was not named Johnny! His name was Roger. Jean's relief was so enormous it left her feeling weak. Those two women were not talking about her at all. They were talking about some other girl. Some other girl entirely. Jean lifted her Coke with hands that still trembled, and took a small sip through her straw. She looked across the table at Sue and saw relief written on her face, too. Jean managed a feeble smile.

"Yes, I suppose girls always will chase him," agreed Fur Piece.

There was no reason why Jean should continue to listen to this conversation, but she was so fascinated she could not help herself.

"It seems to me that Roger is old enough to take care of himself," said Flowery Hat and added, with amusement in her voice, "Are you sure you aren't afraid he likes her?"

"Oh, really!" Fur Piece was impatient.

This exchanged boosted Jean's spirits enough to allow her to look at Sue, who had finished her Coke, with an expressionless face that showed she was concealing what she felt. "Shall we go?" asked Jean.

The girls left the booth and paid their check at the cash register by the candy counter. The gaiety and anticipation that Jean had felt when she entered Snow's was gone, and the fragrance of chocolate now seemed too warm and too sweet. She felt the incident looming between herself and Sue.

"Talk about ups and downs," said Jean, as they walked toward the bus stop. "I have really had it today." When Sue was silent, she burst out, "Why don't you say it? It might as well have been me they were talking about."

"But it wasn't you," Sue's voice was gentle.

"I know." But as they boarded the bus a voice within Jean repeated, It might as well have been you. There was little comfort in knowing she was not the only girl who had chased a boy.

Jean found a seat, clasped her arms around her dress box, and rested her chin on it. She wondered if Johnny really wanted to go to the dance with her after all. What had he said? "Sure, Jean, I'll go with you." As if he was bestowing a favor upon her. And perhaps he was. He knew lots of girls, and she didn't know many boys. It just happened that Johnny was the first boy who had ever paid any attention to her.

And as Jean looked back over the past weeks she realized that the attention Johnny had paid her had not been worth the uneasy vigils in the halls at school, or the ordeal of asking him to go to the dance. Why, trying to find the right moment to ask him to go to the dance had actually spoiled some of her fun in her small part in the variety show. No, Johnny's condescending, "Sure, Jean, I'll go with you," was not worth the strain between herself and Sue, Elaine's hurt feelings, her father's concern.

"Jean, don't feel that way," begged Sue, when they got off the bus. "You are lucky, you know."

"I am?" said Jean. "I thought you didn't like Johnny."

"I don't much," admitted Sue.

"Then why do you say I'm lucky?" asked Jean.

Sue smiled. "When I was fifteen I liked a boy. It seems funny now. He was a tackle on the football team—all chest and not many brains—the kind who stood on the front steps at school and bragged. I thought he was wonderful and cut out his picture every time it was in the paper and tagged him around all semester. He knew I liked him, but nothing ever happened. So you see, you are luckier than I was."

"Why, Sue!" Jean had never suspected her sister of this sort of behavior.

"You were in junior high then," said Sue. "I finally caught on that I really was pretty miserable and that at least half the boys at school didn't even seem to be interested in girls. There didn't seem to be anything anyone could do about it, and I decided next time I would wait for a boy to come along who liked me. Everybody meets somebody sometime, even if it doesn't happen when you are a sophomore. And then one day Kenneth waited for me in the library and everything turned out the way I had dreamed it would. But just the same it would have been nice to have had one date with that tackle."

Jean laughed. "I used to see those clippings from the sport section. I thought it was school spirit, and it really was love."

"Crush is a better word," said Sue. "Or maybe it was rocks in my head or a bee in my bonnet. Anyway, it wasn't love."

As the girls entered their house, Jean thought Sue sounded as if she was sure now that she knew what love was. Jean went into the bedroom and was distracted from her thoughts by the sight of a flat box wrapped in Christmas paper and tied with a red ribbon, lying on her bed. That box, so inappropriate to a warm spring day, saddened Jean. It told her that no matter how she had treated Elaine, Elaine's heart was big enough to want her to have the snapshot of Johnny.

Jean dropped her dress box on the bed, sat down, and read the card on Elaine's package. "Merry Christmas to Jean from Elaine." That was all. No joking remark, no funny note. Carefully Jean untied the ribbon and rolled it up to save for a small package next Christmas. The candy-cane paper, she decided, was not large enough to save, so she tore it off the box. Inside, as she had expected, lay a snapshot on a cushion of crumpled tissue paper. Jean picked it up and studied it. Johnny did look so natural and so handsome as he smiled into the camera. Johnny . . . he was so attractive . . . if *only* . . . Jean broke off that train of thought to study herself in the snapshot. She looked strained as she faced Johnny and at the same time tried to look at the camera—strained and unhappy, and that was how she had felt, too. And that was how she must have appeared to Elaine and Homer and all of Johnny's friends on the steps of the school that day.

"What's that?" asked Sue curiously, as she entered the bedroom.

"Just a joke," answered Jean, rising from the bed and dropping the snapshot into her top drawer. "Just a silly joke." Jean knew then that she no longer wanted to take Johnny to the dance.

CHAPTER 9

Jean, who had found it difficult to invite a boy to go to a dance, found the problem of uninviting him even more difficult. She turned the matter over in her mind all through supper. She was only vaguely conscious of what her father was saying.

"There is this new family on my route," Mr. Jarrett was saying, "with a little boy—he must be about four years old—and this morning he stopped me and said, 'Mr. Mailman, have you seen my dog? He didn't come home last night.' "

Jean was thinking she could hardly go up to Johnny in the hall and say, Excuse me, Johnny, but I don't want to go to the dance with you. A girl couldn't come right out and say a thing like that. She should have an excuse like—like breaking a leg, or being called out of town, or catching the measles.

"And when I reached the bottom of the hill near the end of my route," Mr. Jarrett went on, "another little fellow ran out to meet me. He said, 'Mr. Mailman, see my dog.' He was leading the first little boy's dog by a piece of clothesline tied to its collar."

"What did you do?" asked Sue.

"I had a little talk with the boy's mother. She said she would take the dog back to the first boy in her car, but since her own boy was so happy about the dog, she would get him another."

"A dog that likes mailmen, of course," said Mrs. Jarrett.

Jean smiled absently, more because she was aware her father had finished an anecdote than because she had really listened.

"What's on your mind, Jean?" asked Mr. Jarrett.

"Is something on my mind?" Jean asked, embarrassed that her father had noticed her lack of interest.

"Something is bothering you," answered her father.

Maybe this was one of the times a family could help. "Well . . . I have decided I don't want to take Johnny to the dance after all," said Jean reluctantly, "and I don't know what to do about it."

"But why, dear?" asked Mrs. Jarrett.

"I just don't, is all," answered Jean, searching for an answer to give her mother. "I don't think it would be any fun."

"Of course it would," said Mrs. Jarrett. "Jean, you have to get over being so shy sometime. Sue is having such a good time with Kenneth. I think you should have some fun too."

"Mother, it isn't because I am shy," insisted Jean. "I—I just don't want to go is all. Anyway, it is different with Ken and Sue."

"But, dear, you have asked him and he has accepted," said Mrs. Jarrett. "You can't break a date just because you have changed your mind. How would you feel if a boy treated you that way?"

"He did, sort of," said Jean. "That night he was supposed to come over."

"You don't really know the circumstances of that evening," Mrs. Jarrett pointed out. "There is no reason to believe he wasn't telling the truth."

"I suppose not," said Jean hopelessly. A girl could not tell her mother that she had chased a boy, and that she was hurt by his condescending acceptance of her invitation. Funny little girl. Sure, I'll go with you. How could she explain that?

"You wear your pretty dress and your new shoes and take him to the dance and have a good time," said Mrs. Jarrett.

"Your mother is right—not that I ever thought much of this fellow Johnny," said Jean's father. "But it wouldn't be right to break the date. Take him this time and let that be the end of it. You don't have to go out with him again."

Reluctantly Jean admitted that her mother and father were probably right. Later, in the kitchen, when she and Sue were washing and wiping the supper dishes, Jean whispered, "I couldn't tell them Johnny probably wouldn't even care."

"It will be all right," answered Sue reassuringly. "Four hours isn't forever, and after that you can drop him. Anyway, those women weren't talking about you."

"They might as well have been," said Jean unhappily, as she polished a glass. "You know that."

"You take things too hard," said Sue. "Maybe it

wasn't that way at all. You heard only the woman's version of the story."

"Maybe." When you were fifteen, it seemed difficult to take things any other way.

When the dishes were dried and put away, Jean picked up a letter she had received from her Japanese pen pal that afternoon, and walked over to the Mundys' house to try to make amends for the way she had treated Elaine. "Hi, Elaine," she said, when her friend opened the door. "I thought I would run over and thank you for the Christmas present. You certainly got the pictures developed in a hurry. Wasn't it simply awful of me?"

"Come on in." Elaine seemed glad to see Jean. "It was good of Johnny, though."

Jean saw that Elaine was alone. "Elaine—I'm terribly sorry about the way I treated you the day we took the snapshots. I should have asked you to go around to the playing field too."

"Oh, that's all right," said Elaine. Apologies were as embarrassing to receive as to give.

"Besides," said Jean quickly, to bring an end to the awkward moment, "I brought over a letter I received this afternoon from my Japanese pen pal. I thought you might like to read it. She wants to know if Northgate is near Hollywood. I guess she doesn't realize how big California is."

Elaine took the letter and began to read. "Well, what do you know!" She laughed and looked up from the letter. "She says she is 'particularly interesting in knowing how coeds make date with boys.' Only she spells it d-e-t-e. What are you going to tell her?"

The humorous side of this question had not struck Jean until this moment. "You know, that might be a little difficult to explain," she said, and began to laugh.

Elaine giggled. "You can never explain it in one letter. You will have to write an encyclopedia."

Laughing with Elaine helped to erase Jean's worries. "It would take a whole volume to tell how I made a date with Johnny. And now that I have bought a new dress (at Northgate Apparel, too, by the way) and some pumps with heels, I have changed my mind about wanting to take him."

"You're crazy," said Elaine flatly. "Absolutely mad." Then she added, in a voice that expressed her eagerness for information, "What made you change your mind?"

"I just did," answered Jean vaguely. "I got to thinking that Johnny didn't really care whether he went with me or not."

"But that is not the point," protested Elaine. "The point is that even if you know he doesn't really want to go with you, or even if you don't want to go with him, you should go so that you will be seen. Lots of girls would like to go with Johnny, and everybody knows it. And if you are seen at a school dance with him, everybody will think you rate. And maybe somebody else will ask you the next time."

Perhaps Elaine was right. A girl never would have any fun if she did not make the most of whatever opportunities came her way. But Johnny as an opportunity had not really come Jean's way. She had run after him. Jean wished she were not so uncertain about everything.

"Besides, you have a new dress," Elaine pointed out practically. "And a pair of pumps with heels."

"Yes, there is the dress," agreed Jean. Her lovely plain dress with the shoes tinted to match the sash. Where would she ever wear them if she did not wear them to the dance?

"I think you are lucky," said Elaine. "I don't have

anyone to ask at all. Oh, sure, I know some boys, but if I asked one of them to go to a dance with me he would probably run away screaming."

"Oh, Elaine, don't be silly," said Jean.

"Maybe not screaming exactly," admitted Elaine, "but he would probably be thinking like mad to make up an excuse. I couldn't stand to see him suffer."

"Oh, Elaine," protested Jean, not wanting her friend, who had so many good qualities, to have such a low estimate of herself.

"It's true. I don't know a single boy who would like to go to a dance with me." Whenever Elaine was gloomy she was thoroughly gloomy. "Oh, well, you know me. I always like to see the young people have a good time." Elaine attempted to be jaunty about the whole thing. "You go to the dance and tell me about it."

Laughing at Elaine raised Jean's spirits sufficiently to enable her to decide, I will go. She would go and wear her dress and have what fun she could and after that she would never go out of her way for Johnny again.

"Anyway, things will be better next semester," said Elaine, "because I have decided to learn to play the flute."

"The flute!" Jean could not help laughing. Elaine did have some of the wildest ideas. "How will that help?"

"If I can play the flute I can play in the band," said Elaine. "And the band is full of boys—a lot of them tall. And the band has a lot of fun. It even gets to go on trips sometimes. Maybe none of the boys will notice me, but at least I'll belong to something and be doing something and not just wandering around like a lost soul dreaming about a television singer. Besides, a flute is easy to carry."

"You know, Elaine," said Jean, "I think you have

something there. I haven't felt so left-out since I joined the Costume Club."

Elaine whistled *Yankee Doodle* into an imaginary flute. "Weren't we silly back in the days when we used to dream about Kip Laddish?" she asked, and both girls found this remark extremely funny.

On Monday, after school, Jean, who found that her change in attitude toward Johnny gave her a feeling of independence toward him, did not linger in her clothing classroom in the hope of meeting him on her way out of the building. She managed not to see him at all that day. On Tuesday afternoon he was waiting for her when she came out.

"Oh—hi," said Jean, with more calm than she had ever felt before in speaking to Johnny.

"Hi, there," Johnny answered, looking down at her with a disarming smile. "I've missed you."

"Have you?" answered Jean with composure, while she thought, Have you really, Johnny, or are you just saying it? This new detachment toward Johnny gave her ego a tremendous boost. Who was Johnny Chessler anyway? Just a boy.

"Say . . . Jean," Johnny hesitated, and then, leaning lazily against a locker, smiled down at her. "I know you aren't going to believe what I am going to say."

Jean returned his smile. "Probably not," she said lightly. Even though her feelings toward him had changed, she still found him attractive.

"My grandmother is pretty sick," said Johnny, "and I am not going to be able to go to the dance Saturday night. Dad says it wouldn't be right for me to go when she is so sick, and all."

Jean felt her face turn scarlet. Why, *why* hadn't she broken the date first? Now no one would ever believe she had wanted to break it, even if she told anyone, which, of course, now she could never do. His grandmother! Jean was suddenly more angry than hurt, not because he was breaking the date, but because he was offering such a flimsy excuse.

"Anyone with your imagination should be able to think up a better excuse," she told him.

"See?" said Johnny. "You don't believe me, do you?"

"No, Johnny," said Jean levelly. "I don't believe you, but it is all right. You don't have to go to the dance with me."

Surprise flickered across Johnny's face. He had expected Jean to show disappointment, to protest, perhaps to plead. That glimpse of surprise helped to support Jean's pride. "And now I am going to tell you something *you* won't believe," she said, pleased with her unexpected poise. "I have been wanting to break the date with you." She noted more than a flicker of surprise on Johnny's face.

Johnny smiled his lazy smile. "How come?" he asked. "How come you have changed your mind?"

Jean looked Johnny straight in the eye. "Because I have thought it over and decided I don't want to go with you, because you don't really want to go with me."

"You have more spunk than I thought you had." Johnny grinned, and ran the tip of his finger down Jean's nose. "And you know something?" he drawled. "You're cute when you're mad."

Oh! "I'm glad you think so," answered Jean and, turning, walked away from Johnny with her head held high. Let him laugh if he wanted to. Johnny, she was sure, would not believe her, because it would be difficult for Johnny to believe any girl did not like him. Nevertheless, she felt better for speaking the words.

Jean hurried down the hall to Elaine's locker.

"Why—hello." Elaine sounded surprised. "I thought you would be waiting for Johnny."

"I'm through waiting for Johnny," answered Jean.

"You didn't break the date after all?" asked Elaine, as she snapped shut the padlock of her locker.

"No, I didn't break it," said Jean. "Johnny did."

Elaine turned to face Jean. "Oh, Jean! How awful."

"It isn't awful at all," said Jean calmly. "You know I didn't want to go with him. And now I don't have to."

"But to have *him* break it—" Elaine was so outraged she did not finish the sentence. "I mean, a girl has her pride. He can't treat you that way." Elaine scowled, and said urgently, "Jean, you've got to go to that dance. You've *got* to go and wear your dress, just to show Johnny! It is bound to get back to him that you went to the dance after all."

Jean doubted this, but she felt herself infected by the intensity of Elaine's feelings. "But who could I ask?"

"There must be somebody," said Elaine. "*Think.* Think hard."

"I'm thinking," said Jean, "but it doesn't help." There was that boy in her English class who had been friendly, but he had already been asked, she knew. And a boy in math—no, she didn't know him well enough and besides, she thought he was already going steady. And of course there were no boys at all in Clothing or in the Costume Club.

"What about one of the Indians from the variety show?" suggested Elaine.

"No," said Jean. "There was such a bunch of them that I don't remember any one especially."

"Homer!" said Elaine triumphantly.

"Homer?" echoed Jean.

"He's a boy and he knows you," said Elaine.

"Yes, but—Homer. I never thought of him as a boy to dance with," protested Jean.

"You can start," Elaine informed her.

So Jean leaned back against a locker, her books clutched in her arms, and thought about Homer as a boy to take to a dance. It was not easy, because she had always thought of him as a boy who tagged around after Johnny. Or used to. Now that she thought about it, she had not seen them together lately.

"He's not really homely, or anything like that," Elaine pointed out. "And he shouldn't mind your glasses, because he wears glasses himself. And he has nice manners. He isn't anybody you would be ashamed to be seen with."

"N-no," said Jean. He was not anyone she was especially eager to be seen with, either. Still, there was nothing actually wrong with him now that she took the trouble to think about him. Perhaps the only thing wrong with Homer was that he was so easy not to think about. Like me, thought Jean. I am awfully easy for boys not to think about.

"Remember your dress and your high heels," said Elaine, as if she were dangling bait in front of Jean.

Jean was tempted. "What if he has a date?"

"He won't have," said Elaine confidently. "Go on, Jean. Ask him for—for the sake of womanhood. You don't want to be downtrodden by someone like Johnny, do you?"

Jean could not help laughing. "Oh, Elaine, the way you put things! All right. I'll ask him for the sake of womanhood. The worst he can do is turn me down."

"Good!" Elaine was jubilant. "You'd better ask him right away."

"Before I lose my courage?" asked Jean.

"Partly," admitted Elaine, "and because you can't wait until the day of the dance to ask him. It wouldn't look right."

"Elaine, I can't telephone him." Jean did not think she could ever bring herself to telephone a boy again.

"Ask him the first thing in the morning and *don't change your mind*."

"I won't." Jean sounded less certain than her promise. Together the girls walked down the hall. Jean found it pleasant to be walking the familiar route with Elaine once more, instead of lingering outside her clothing classroom, hoping that Johnny's whim might bring him toward her. She had never found any real pleasure in those uncertain moments, and now she wondered why she had waited at all. She felt as if she had suddenly been set free. As they passed the foot of the central stairs, both girls saw Homer descending from the library, a book in his hand.

"Here's your chance," whispered Elaine, and disappeared.

Here goes, thought Jean, glad that she would not have time to change her mind. "Hi, Homer," she said, when he had reached the bottom of the stairs.

"Hello, Jean," Homer answered. He hesitated and then started to walk down the hall.

"Homer—could I talk to you a minute?" Jean asked nervously.

"Why sure, Jean." Homer turned back.

"Homer—" Jean had to force herself to utter the words. "Homer, would you go to the Girls' Association Dance with me?" The invitation was offered, and now the worst that could happen was his refusal. She could take it bravely if she had to.

"Why—" Homer's face turned crimson.

Just the way mine does sometimes, thought Jean.

Homer's face relaxed into a smile. "Why—sure, Jean," he answered, looking flustered. "Gosh, that would be *swell!*"

"Swell," said Jean, weak with relief.

"I mean—that would really be *swell*," said Homer.

He honestly means it, thought Jean. How different was his reaction from Johnny's . . . and how pleasant

it was to watch. Jean and Homer looked at one another and this time Jean really observed him. He is a
nice boy, she thought, and he has long eyelashes behind his glasses. She felt ashamed that she had not
taken the trouble to look at him before.

"Golly, I never expected a girl to ask *me* to go to a
dance," Homer blurted out.

Jean was touched by Homer's humility. Then she
remembered Johnny, and wondered if Homer knew
she had asked him first. If he did not already know,
he was sure to hear it. Jean did not want this boy's
feelings to be hurt. She bit her lip for a moment while
she decided that the best thing to do was to tell him
herself. Right now.

"Uh . . . Homer," she began. "I guess maybe I had
better confess. I asked Johnny first and then he—he
broke the date."

If Homer was disappointed, he concealed his feelings from Jean. "That's O.K.," he said awkwardly. "I
guess there are some fellows who just naturally get
asked first."

"I don't suppose anybody will believe me, but I was
sorry I had asked him and I really wanted to break the
date myself," Jean explained. "I mean, I am not heart-
broken or anything like that because he broke the
date." Naturally a boy would not enjoy going to a
dance with a girl whose heart was breaking over another boy.

"That Johnny!" was all Homer said.

"My mother will drive us," said Jean. "I'm not old
enough to get a license."

"That's all right. She doesn't need to go to that
trouble," said Homer. "I can get our car."

"Could you really?" asked Jean. It would be lots
more fun to go in the boy's car.

"Sure," said Homer. "I'll be glad to."

Jean did not know what to do with the conversation next. Homer had accepted and he would supply the transportation. There seemed nothing more to discuss.

"I'm sure glad you asked me," said Homer, "even if I wasn't first."

The wonderful part was, he meant it.

"Well, I have to go now," said Jean. "I'll probably see you before Friday."

"Sure," said Homer. "I'll see you around school."

As they parted Jean turned to watch this boy walk down the hall. There was no mistaking it. His walk was jauntier than she had ever seen it before. Elaine was by her side, seeming to appear from nowhere.

"What did you do?" asked Jean. "Disappear in a puff of smoke?"

"I went into the nearest room. I thought it was the right moment for me to tactfully disappear," Elaine explained. "Did he say yes?"

"That's right." Jean looked thoughtfully at Homer, who was going out the door at the end of the hall.

"Hooray!" exclaimed Elaine. "That will show old Johnny."

Jean wondered. Probably Johnny would not even know, because the activities of the Jeans and Homers were scarcely news around Northgate High. And if he did find out, she doubted very much that he would care.

"Tell me about it." Elaine was always impatient for details. "He didn't just say yes and walk off. What happened?"

"You know something, Elaine?" said Jean wonderingly. "He *wants* to go to the dance with me. He really does."

"And now you can wear the dress!" Elaine sighed happily. "And the heels."

"Yes, I can wear my dress," said Jean dreamily.

Maybe Homer wasn't a boy she would have chosen to take to the dance if she had had the whole school to choose from, but he was a boy who really wanted to go with her. He was actually enthusiastic and wasn't afraid to show it. Jean smiled to herself. Maybe Homer wasn't the handsomest boy in school or the most popular. She didn't care. He was a nice boy and he was eager, really eager to go to the dance with her. And that, Jean discovered, made up for a lot of things.

CHAPTER
10

Jean practiced wearing her brown linen pumps. She walked across the carpet, she walked on the bare floor. She danced forward, she danced backward, she whirled in circles, and all the while the phrase, "She walks in beauty," whispered through her thoughts.

Mr. Jarrett rubbed the soles of Jean's new shoes with sandpaper and, feeling more secure, she wore the shoes every possible moment until it was time to dress for the dance. Without her saddle shoes she felt light enough to float. It was a joy to slip into the new dress, now shortened to a becoming length, and have Sue pull up the long zipper for her. Carefully she knotted the brown-and-apricot sash.

"Your turn for the mirror," said Sue, who had had first turn at the bathroom and who had now finished dressing. She and Kenneth were going to drive across the bay to see some old movies that were part of a series called "The Development of the Motion Picture as an Art," which was being shown at a museum. "You look darling and I hope you have a wonderful time with Homer."

Jean smiled into the mirror at her sister, who seemed to shine with happiness tonight. "Thank you. And I don't have to hope you will have a good time. I know you will." She combed her bangs into place before she asked, "You really like Kenneth, don't you?"

"Mm-hm," answered Sue. "He's—he just wonderful, that's all."

"I'm glad," said Jean sincerely and wistfully. It would be so nice if she could feel that Homer was wonderful too.

The doorbell rang. "He's here!" Sue snatched her coat from the closet, and was gone.

Jean enjoyed having the bedroom to herself. She fluffed the ends of her hair and admired her dress all over again. Johnny and the clerk in Northgate Apparel were right. She was attractive. It was funny, too, because she had the same brown hair and the same too short nose that she had always had, and yet now she was different. She felt attractive. Maybe wearing glasses and being too short did not matter as much as she had believed. I am attractive, she told herself. I believe it now. But in the back of Jean's mind lurked an unhappy thought. If she was attractive, why didn't Johnny want to go to the dance with her?

"Jean, why don't you come out and let us see how you look?" Mrs. Jarrett called from the living room.

Feeling suddenly shy in front of her mother and father, Jean made her entrance.

Mr. Jarrett whistled.

"You look lovely, dear," said Mrs. Jarrett. "That dress is most becoming."

"Thank you," said Jean. It was comforting to know her family was proud of her.

"And I can tell you one thing," said Mr. Jarrett.

"That fellow Johnny is going to be sorry he changed his mind."

"No danger," said Jean. "He won't be there."

"Not that I ever thought he amounted to a hill of beans," said Mr. Jarrett, as he reached into his pocket and pulled out his wallet. He took out two one-dollar bills and handed them to Jean. "Since this is a girls' affair, you had better take this along. A boy gets pretty hungry dancing."

"Thank you, Daddy." It was thoughtful of her father to do this and just before payday, too. Jean took the money into the bedroom and slipped it into the pocket of her coat—really her mother's coat, borrowed for the occasion. Maybe Homer would like to go to the drive-in after the dance, because that was where everybody went.

The doorbell rang for the second time that evening. Where had the moments flown? Jean had not had time to start being nervous about Homer's arrival, and here he was already. She snatched up the coat which she dropped on a chair in the living room, and hurried to open the door. "Hello, Homer," she said. "Won't you come in and meet my mother and father?"

Jean, who had rehearsed this introduction in her mind for several days, managed it smoothly. Reading approval on the faces of her parents, she tried to view Homer through their eyes and saw a serious-looking boy in a white shirt and gray flannel suit, with his hair mowed short. Because he was wearing a necktie he looked more grown-up than he looked at school, and he was quite at ease with her parents, which surprised Jean. Somehow, she had expected him to blush and stammer.

"Shall we go, Jean?" Homer asked, as he picked up her coat.

"Have a good time, children," said Mrs. Jarrett, as Homer put his hand on the doorknob. Jean, who was often annoyed with her mother for what she considered the careless use of the word *children*, did not mind this time. It was a loving word, the way her mother spoke it, and Jean felt that now her mother was extending her warm feelings to include this boy who was happy to go to the dance with her daughter.

"Take good care of my daughter," said Mr. Jarrett.

"Oh, Dad," laughed Jean, embarrassed by her father's remark.

"I will, sir," said Homer seriously.

Jean experienced a pleasant feeling of being cherrished. After she had walked successfully down the steps in her high heels, and she and Homer were seated in the car, he handed her a clear plastic florist's box that protected one perfect white camellia. "I know this isn't a formal dance or anything like that," he said bashfully, "but, I—uh—thought you might like a flower anyway."

"Why, Homer—" A boy had given her a flower! "Homer, it's lovely!" Jean would never have guessed that Homer was the kind of boy who would give a girl a flower.

"Do you really like it?" asked Homer, as he started the car. "I wasn't sure whether it was the thing to do or not."

"I love it," said Jean. This waxy camellia was more than a perfect blossom to Jean. It was thoughtfulness boxed in plastic, and after Johnny, Jean found a boy's thoughtfulness a lovely thing to hold in her two hands. She held the gift carefully all the way to the gymnasium, where she left the box (which of course she wanted to keep forever) in the car. After she had checked her coat she pinned the camellia to her dress with the stem up, took it off, and repinned it with the stem down.

When Jean joined Homer at the edge of the dance floor and handed him her coat check, she was suddenly frightened. "Homer, maybe I should tell you," she said hesitantly, listening to the beat of the orchestra. "I'm not a very good dancer."

"Neither am I," Homer confessed cheerfully. "Not this kind of dancing. I'm pretty good at folk dancing."

Nevertheless, Jean felt her palms grow cold as Homer dropped her coat check into his pocket. Her mouth felt as dry as Kleenex and she made an excuse to step over to the drinking fountain. The water seemed the most delicious she had ever tasted. She longed to postpone the moment when she had to step onto the dance floor, but they had come to dance, and dance they must. Fortunately there were not many couples on the floor yet, so there would not be many people to bump into. And Jean had the satisfaction of knowing that she was becomingly dressed. That helped a lot.

Homer put his arm around Jean, took her hand, and together they moved onto the floor. Almost immediately Jean stumbled. "Excuse me," they both said at the same time, and laughed nervously.

They started to dance again. Homer stepped squarely on the toe of Jean's new pumps.

"Excuse me," repeated Homer, "but you are always supposed to start with your right foot. I start with my left."

"Oh, excuse me," apologized Jean, recalling that Elaine had told her this. They began actually to move along with the other couples. Homer's hand, Jean discovered, was as cold as hers, and she took comfort in knowing that a boy could be nervous too. They stumbled once more, and both said, "Excuse me."

"Look," said Homer. "Let's lay a few ground rules. No more apologies. We'll just do the best we can."

Jean felt a wild desire to giggle, but when they had circled the gymnasium floor once, she had a real sense of achievement. We made it, she thought triumphantly. When the music stopped she surreptitiously rubbed her cold, moist hand on her skirt. Homer, she noticed, rubbed his hand on his coat.

"Look," said Homer once more. "Maybe I shouldn't say it, but couldn't you sort of relax? I am supposed to do the leading, you know."

"I'll try," said Jean contritely. Dancing with a boy was a lot different from dancing with Elaine. When the music began once more, Jean tried to be limp.

"That's better," said Homer.

Jean was encouraged, but gradually as she danced she felt herself stiffen. Relax, she told herself sternly and managed to be less tense. Homer's dancing, she soon discovered, was as regular as the beat of a metronome. When she could be sure he would not try any unexpected steps, she felt encouraged and even glanced at him. Why, he shaves, she thought. How silly of her! Of course he shaved. He was a senior and must be seventeen. She somehow had never thought of him as old enough to have a beard. Should they, she began to wonder, be carrying on a conversation?

"I thought there would be a larger crowd," she said experimentally, not at all sure she could dance and talk at the same time.

"It will get larger later," explained Homer. "It is the herd instinct in reverse. Half the crowd is afraid to come before nine for fear they might be the first ones here."

Jean wondered how Homer knew this. Around and around the floor they circled. Jean's feet, unaccustomed to high heels, began to hurt. She thought perhaps she should have bought a larger pair of shoes and caught herself leaning heavily on Homer's shoulder to relieve the pressure on her toes. Quickly she straightened. Her poor, poor toes.

When the music stopped, Jean slipped off one shoe and wiggled her toes. *Ahh.* Bliss. Pure bliss. Now for the first time Jean was able to look around her. She noticed on the bleachers a number of pairs of girls' shoes, and when she looked at the girls on the dance floor, she discovered many had been dancing in their stocking feet.

"That crunching sound you have been hearing," remarked Homer, "is the sound of toes being stepped on."

Jean could not help admiring the girls who were such good dancers they could risk their toes. When the music started, Jean managed to shove her foot into her shoe, which was a size too small. Around and around they danced, repeating the same steps over and over. Jean began to feel that she was getting to know Homer's gray flannel shoulder very well. Around and around. There was no hope of a change of scenery, because no one traded dances as Jean had expected. Around and around. Either Jean's feet were growing or her shoes were shrinking. The whole situation suddenly struck Jean as being hilariously funny and she wanted to laugh. Politeness, however, prevented her from showing how she felt. School dances weren't supposed to be funny. Naturally she could not let Homer know that she thought it was ridiculous to dance around and around with one gray flannel shoulder. She began to wonder how many laps around the gymnasium made a mile.

Suddenly Jean stiffened and was aware that Homer had not only noticed her quick intake of breath but was staring in the same direction, toward the checkroom door, where Johnny was standing with Peggy Jo. Johnny was looking intently at Peggy Jo, who was almost as tall as he was. She said something, and they both laughed. Then Johnny put his arm around Peggy Jo and they began to dance, easily and gracefully.

The pleasure was completely drained from Jean's evening, which had begun to seem like a private joke that she had been enjoying in spite of her toes. All that was gone, now that she knew Johnny thought so little of her that he would break a date to go with another girl. Did he think she was such a—a mouse that she could not ask another boy? Or didn't he care? And what was she supposed to do now? She could not face Johnny. That she knew.

"Did you think he wouldn't come?" asked Homer mildly.

"I guess so," admitted Jean, stumbling on Homer's foot. Don't let Johnny see me, she thought fervently. Just don't let him see me. She danced with her eyes on Homer's shoulder, hoping that if she could avoid seeing Johnny, that somehow he would not see her. Each step was more painful than the one before, and when the music stopped, Jean stood on her right foot and wiggled the toes of her left foot while she stared wretchedly at the basketball foul-line painted on the floor.

"You don't want to see Johnny, do you?" asked Homer bluntly.

Jean stood on her left foot and wiggled the toes on her right foot. "No," she confessed shamefacedly.

"Why?" asked Homer. "He should be embarrassed. Not you."

Why? How could a girl explain to a boy that it was humiliating not to be wanted, and even more humiliating that a boy did not care about her feelings. And yet she knew Homer was right. "I just feel funny about it, is all," Jean said lamely. Thoughtful Homer, who had been kind enough to bring her a flower— Jean had to think of him, too. She could not spoil his evening, when he had been so glad to come with her.

Jean smiled shakily, and the music started once more. When Jean caught a glimpse of Johnny on the other side of the gymnasium, she found herself smothering a ridiculous feeling of wistfulness. It would be so wonderful to be dancing with a tall, good-looking boy like Johnny, a boy whose dancing was graceful and not like the beat of a metronome. If only Johnny had been some other kind of boy. . . .

The music stopped and inevitably, when Homer dropped Jean's hand, she found herself facing Johnny. She could not miss the surprise, followed by embarrassment, that crossed Johnny's handsome face. So he hadn't thought she had enough spirit to ask another boy to go to the dance. Well, she would show him! "Hello, Johnny," she said coolly. "Hello, Peggy Jo."

"Why—hello, Jean," answered Johnny. There was an awkward pause. Peggy Jo smiled, apparently unaware of the situation.

"Hi, Johnny," said Homer.

Jean felt a little wicked. "Isn't it miraculous the things they do with wonder drugs these days?" she asked, looking directly at Johnny.

"Wonder drugs?" Johnny did not know what she was talking about.

"Yes. Your grandmother—I am so glad she is feeling better," said Jean with a smile.

"Uh—yes," said Johnny, and Jean was happy to see that he was embarrassed.

"Jean, would you like some punch?" asked Homer.

"Yes, thank you," answered Jean. The uncomfortable moment was over. She had been able to face Johnny after all. Her relief was followed by an unexpected feeling of gaiety, as she accompanied Homer to the little grass shack made out of crepe paper, and accepted a paper cup of pineapple punch from Homer. It was so cold and refreshing that for an instant Jean wished she could pour it over her toes.

"What was that about wonder drugs?" Homer asked.

"Oh, that—" Jean laughed. "Johnny used a sick

grandmother as an excuse for breaking his date with me, and I couldn't resist reminding him of it."

When Homer threw back his head and laughed, Jean laughed with him. Over his shoulder Jean caught a glimpse of Johnny looking toward them, as if he was surprised to see them enjoying themselves. What did Johnny expect me to do, Jean thought in annoyance. Sob my little heart out? She smiled warmly at Homer.

Homer drained his cup of punch before he spoke. "Jean, let's face it. We aren't having a good time."

"Why, Homer—" In her consternation, Jean did not know what to say. She felt as if she had failed, because everyone who came to a dance was supposed to have a good time. That was what dances were for. "Homer, I am terribly sorry."

"What are you sorry about?" Homer asked. "There's nothing so terrible about that, is there? Maybe we just aren't the kind of people who have a good time at a dance. I think it is pretty stupid myself, the way a lot of people come and don't dance at all, or don't trade dances. I belong to a folk-dance group that is lots more fun than this, because everybody mixes."

Jean found that in her heart she agreed with Homer, but what could they do if they left the dance now? It was only nine-thirty. Nobody went home at nine-thirty. It even seemed too early to suggest going to the drive-in.

"Look, Jean," said Homer eagerly. "Would you like to see my pigeons?"

"Your pigeons?" repeated Jean. What on earth was Homer talking about now?

"Yes. My homing pigeons. I have six in a cote in the back yard at home," Homer explained.

"I didn't know you kept pigeons." Jean was stalling for time to think. She wanted to leave the dance, but she wondered what her mother and father would say about her going to a boy's house. She had no idea, the problem was so unexpected.

"It would be all right for you to come," said Homer. "Mom and Dad are home. The have some friends there."

This settled the problem in Jean's mind. "I would love to see your pigeons, Homer," she said.

"Swell," said Homer. "Let's get your coat."

As they left the checkroom, Johnny and Peggy Jo danced by. Johnny grinned lazily at Jean over Peggy Jo's shoulder, and winked. Oh, stop it, Johnny, thought Jean, and repinned her camellia to her coat, stem up this time.

When they climbed into the car, Jean realized that she did not even know where Homer lived. How heavenly it was to be able to take off both her shoes! They drove through the business district and took a road that wound uphill, twisting and turning until at last Homer drove up a steep driveway. Jean had to shove to get her shoes back on again. As they got out of the car Jean paused to look at the lights of the city below and of the cities in the distance strung together by necklaces of lights on the bridges across the bay. Jean breathed deeply. It was good to be out of the gymnasium, which always smelled faintly of sneakers and sweeping compound, and into the night air, so much cooler up here in the hills and scented with eucalyptus.

"Come on in and meet Mom and Dad while I get the flashlight," said Homer, leading Jean toward the front door.

"Well, you are home early," remarked Mr. Darvey, when Homer had taken Jean into the living room and introduced her to his parents and their guests.

"I wanted to show Jean my pigeons," said Homer. He seemed at ease in a roomful of adults—much more at ease than he ever appeared at school.

"But the dance can't be over this early." Mrs. Darvey was concerned over her son's early return. "What happened?"

"Jean and I decided we would rather look at pigeons," said Homer easily. "Come on, Jean." He led her into the kitchen, where he found a flashlight in a drawer. They went out the back door and walked across a lighted patio.

Jean had an impression of blooming rhododendrons and azaleas and, beneath the flowering shrubs, masses of blue and yellow violas. "What a lovely garden," remarked Jean, as she followed Homer along a path that led into the dark.

"Mom's a spring-garden fiend," said Homer, lighting the way for Jean. "Nothing much blooms the rest of the year, but it is sure beautiful now. Mom says the seasons are so indefinite in California that she tries to make up for it with a good rousing springtime."

Under a cluster of eucalyptus trees they came to the pigeon cote, a neat structure stained gray to match the house. Homer opened the door and flashed the light inside. Six sleeping pigeons stirred on their perches, blinked, and flapped their wings. Homer reached inside and brought out one pigeon. "This is Papa Pigeon," he said. "Would you like to hold him?"

Jean took the uneasy pigeon in her arms and gently stroked the iridescent feathers.

"Papa Pigeon is the father of those two," said Homer, pointing. "And that one is Mama Pigeon." He lifted out another bird. "This one we call Ugh. He was the first squab I raised, and when he hatched he was the weirdest thing I had ever seen. He had a great big beak, all out of proportion to his skinny little body, and his skin was covered with yellow hair. But he grew fast and is a beauty now."

"And do they really come home?" asked Jean.

"Always," said Homer. "We have a lot of fun on

Sundays when we go for a drive. We take them along and release them in the country, and no matter which way we take them, they always circle around for a while and then head for home in the right direction."

One by one Homer removed the pigeons for Jean to stroke. She had not realized how soft and smooth feathers were. "Just like satin," she murmured, running her hand down a glossy back. "Smoother than satin." The pigeon flapped its wings and for a moment Jean was afraid it might slip out of her fingers. Homer took it from her and returned it to the perch. "And did you build the pigeon cote?" she asked.

"Last summer," answered Homer. "I drew up the plans and Dad helped me build it." He closed and fastened the door of the cote and led the way back toward the house.

Jean put her hand in her pocket and felt the money her father had given her to treat Homer. "Homer," she said hesitantly, "would you like to go to the drive-in? I mean, I made the date and I—I would like to treat you."

"Let's not go to that crummy place," said Homer. "Come on in the house and I'll make you a milk shake."

"All right." At first Jean was a little hurt by Homer's rejection of her invitation, but the more she thought about it, the more she began to feel that Homer was right about the drive-in. She began to feel a kind of admiration for this boy who would come right out and say he did not like the most popular meeting place of high-school students, and who saw nothing wrong with leaving a dance he did not enjoy. Jean had alway felt critical of herself because she was not like everyone else at school

In the kitchen Homer took Jean's coat after she had unpinned her camellia. "What kind of milk shake would you like?" he asked.

"I like any kind," answered Jean, as she pinned the camellia, stem down, to her dress. She would not like to say she liked chocolate milk shakes if the Darveys did not have any chocolate syrup.

While Homer was opening the refrigerator, Jean looked around at the kitchen, which was larger than the Jarretts'. Instead of curtains, the windows had shades, made of pink-and-white striped ticking. I must tell Mother, thought Jean. Shades like that, instead of curtains, were attractive and would save a lot of ironing, too. Her mother could watch for a remnant of pink-and-white ticking . . . or yellow-and-white might look prettier in their kitchen. . . .

Homer removed a carton of ice cream and a box of strawberries from the refrigerator. "We have bananas, too," he said, "and there is a dish of pineapple in here if you like pineapple milk shakes."

"They all sound good," said Jean.

"I'll tell you what I'll do," said Homer. "I'll use all three." He spooned ice cream into an electric blender and added a banana, a few strawberries, and a slice of pineapple. He flipped the switch, let the blender whir a moment, and poured two milk shakes into two tall glasses. "We even have straws," he said, opening a cupboard.

"Paper-covered straws!" exclaimed Jean.

"That's right," said Homer. "All the comforts of a soda fountain." He sat down at the table across from Jean, and together they peeled the paper from their straws and began to sip their milk shakes.

"Mmm. Good." said Jean. "Banana-strawberry-pineapple milk shakes are my very favorite from now on." It was fun to be sitting in a kitchen that looked like a magazine illustration, drinking a milk shake that a boy had made. "You are right about the drive-in," she said. "It is a crummy place. I just never thought of it that way, because . . . well, everybody goes there. I guess I thought liking the drive-in was compulsory."

"You sure look nice in that dress," said Homer.

"Why—thank you, Homer." Jean had not expected him to be the kind of boy who would notice a girl's dress.

"I like it because it is sort of streamlined," said Homer seriously. "It isn't a lot of material cluttered up with stuff."

Even though Jean laughed at Homer's masculine description of her dress, she found it pleasant to have a boy appreciate her appearance.

"The color is nice too," said Homer. "Plain and not a lot of swirls and swooshes and little pink rosebuds, like most girls wear."

Jean smiled at him over her milk shake. "I am sure my sewing teacher would like to hear you describe girls' dresses."

"Maybe I don't know the right words, but I know what I like." Homer grinned at Jean and smoothed out the paper wrapper of one of the straws, which he handed to Jean. "Here is a souvenir for you."

"Thank you," she said gravely. There was something she very much wanted to ask Homer. She thought it over a moment and decided there was no reason why she shouldn't ask. "Homer, tell me something. You and Johnny used to be friends. What happened?"

"Sure we were friends." There was some bitterness in Homer's voice. "My dad lets me take the car and Johnny's dad won't. Oh, sure, I know I used to think he was great and tagged around after him and all. He was popular and I guess I thought some of it would rub off on me."

"But he took me out in his car once," said Jean.

"Just once, and I'll bet it was in the daytime," said Homer. "His mother lets him take her car when his dad isn't home. He had his license taken away because a cop picked him up for doing ninety on the freeway."

"Johnny drove ninety miles an hour on the freeway!" Jean was shocked.

"And then Johnny got sore at me that night he asked to come over to see you. He wanted me to go along and I wouldn't. I figured he asked you for a date, and you wouldn't want me coming along, too."

"That stormy night," reminisced Jean. "I remember it rained all day."

"And he said he didn't want to walk to your house in the rain," Homer went on, "and I said that was his problem. Johnny got sore, and after that he didn't bother about me." Homer grinned across the table at Jean. "I'll bet he was sopping when he got there."

Jean bit her lip and looked into her empty glass. "He didn't get there, Homer," she said quietly, hurt because Johnny had not been willing to go through rain and gloom of night to see her. She could not help thinking of her father, who delivered mail in all kinds of weather and even gave extra service to the people on his route without complaining.

"I'm sorry, Jean," said Homer. "I didn't know. Like I said, after that Johnny was sore at me and I didn't think so much of him, either. And I got to thinking about a lot of things. Things like what was so wonderful about a fellow like Johnny and what was so wonderful about being popular. There are lots more interesting things to do besides hanging around a drive-in or cruising around town in a car."

"Homer, does Peggy Jo have her own car?" Jean asked suddenly. "It seems to me I heard someone say something about it during the rehearsal of the variety show."

"Yes, she does," answered Homer. "A hard top."

"Oh." That explained a lot to Jean. Johnny did not

want to bother going to a dance with a girl whose mother had to drive them. Now that she knew the real reason he had broken the date, the unhappy question lurking in the back of her mind was banished.

"What are we talking about Johnny for?" Homer demanded. "Johnny is Johnny's greatest admirer."

Why, that is true, thought Jean. Johnny liked Johnny, and the reason he had liked her was that she had been a good audience. An audience was important to Johnny, she realized, now that she looked back on the last few months, and she had certainly hung on every word he spoke. "Yes, let's not talk about Johnny.'" Jean unwound the wrapper of the straw from her finger. "Maybe I should be starting home. Dad said I had to be in by midnight." Since she and Homer had left the dance, time had gone surprisingly fast. Jean had heard the Darveys' guests leave some time ago.

"Sure, Jean," said Homer with a grin. "I promised your father I would take good care of you."

In the living room, while Homer got her coat, Jean said good night to Mr. and Mrs. Darvey.

"Good night, Jean," said Mrs. Darvey. "I am so glad Homer brought you home. I hope you will come again."

"Thank you." Jean smiled shyly at this woman who liked a good rousing springtime. She could tell that Homer's mother and father liked her. Awkwardly she unfastened the camellia from her dress and pinned it to her coat.

When Homer turned the car into the Jarretts' driveway, he turned off the motor and switched off the lights. Jean waited for him to get out of the car, but when he did not, they sat in silence. Jean began to feel uncomfortable. Her mother and father and the people next door must have heard them drive in and might be thinking that Jean, on her first date, was parked in the driveway with a boy.

"The people next door just had their house painted," said Jean to break the silence, even though she knew Homer would not be interested.

Homer did not answer.

"I mean—you can still smell the paint," said Jean, because a girl had to say something at a time like this. "I thought you might have noticed it."

Homer laid his arm across the back of the seat and turned to Jean. "Jean," he said earnestly, "would you consider kissing me?"

"*Kissing* you!" The words were startled out of Jean. What a funny idea—kissing Homer. Jean's impulse was to jump out of the car and run up the steps into the house.

"Yes," said Homer seriously. "I wondered if you would be interested."

Interested! Homer made kissing sound as impersonal as—as discussing a current event. Jean could not imagine kissing Homer. And if she did, with both of them wearing glasses there would be an unromantic clash of spectacle frames. Or did couples who both wore glasses say, Excuse me while I remove my glasses? And if they did, *then* what did they do? Hold them? Or pull out their cases, fold their glasses, and put them away, saying, Now I am ready to be kissed. Had Homer thought of this, she wondered. The way he was behaving, they would probably have an impersonal discussion of the problem. Jean, he would say, since you have agreed to kiss me, perhaps we should remove our glasses. Yes, Homer, she would answer, that is an excellent suggestion. *Oh*. What was she thinking of anyway? She wasn't going to kiss Homer.

"Well?" said Homer. "You haven't answered."

"Why I . . ." Jean did not know what to say. She

did not want to hurt his feelings, because she liked him. And anyway, she had probably already hurt his feelings by sounding horrified when he mentioned kissing. She had not meant to sound that way, but in her surprise she could not help it. "I mean . . . Well, no thank you. What I mean is, this is just our first date and everything—" Jean stopped. Would he think she expected him to ask her for a second date? Or would he—this was worse—think she was leading him on? What was a girl supposed to do at a moment like this? She wished she knew.

"I didn't think you would," said Homer seriously, "but I didn't think it would hurt to ask."

"No, I guess it doesn't hurt to ask," said Jean, so relieved to get through this awkward moment that she felt for the second time that evening a wild desire to giggle. Elaine would die laughing. Except that this time she was not going to tell Elaine, because even though she thought the situation was funny, there was something so likable about Homer that she would not want anyone to make fun of him. Not ever.

A square of light from a bedroom window fell on the driveway, telling Jean that her father must have turned on the bedroom light to look at the time. The car clock said ten minutes to midnight.

"Homer, I think I had better go in," said Jean.

Homer got out of the car, went around, and opened the door for her. This time Jean could not bear to shove her feet into her pumps. She picked up her shoes and her florist's box and stepped out of the car in her stocking feet. The walked up the steps and when Jean had unlatched the door she stood with one hand on the knob. Her parents, she was sure, would hear the click of the lock and know that she was about to come in. "Thank you for going to the dance with me," she said, feeling that this was proper, because she had extended the invitation. With etiquette out of the way, she laughed and said, "I know the dance was pretty awful, but I really did have a good time at your house. I loved seeing your pigeons and the milk shake was fun, too."

"I'm sure glad you asked me," answered Homer. Then he hesitated. "Jean—would you like to go out again sometime? With me, I mean?"

"Yes, Homer, I would," answered Jean.

"Swell." Homer sounded both pleased and relieved. "Maybe next Saturday afternoon we could take the pigeons out over the hills and release them."

"I would love to. And I—I hope your feelings aren't hurt, or anything, because I didn't—" ventured Jean, and stopped.

"That's all right." Homer understood what she was talking about. "Good night, Jean."

"Good night, Homer. And thank you again for the flower." Jean stepped into the living room, closed the door, started to turn off the light, remembered that Sue probably had not come in, and walked in her stocking feet to the kitchen, where she removed the bruised camellia from her coat and laid it next to a carton of eggs in the refrigerator. Then she tiptoed into the bedroom, sat down on the bed, and began to rub one aching foot.

So that was the way it was, Jean thought. A girl went out with a boy she did not much care about, and her evening did not turn out at all the way she had imagined. In many ways it was disappointing, even painful, and yet when it was over, it was all right. She liked the boy and he liked her. And she would be happy to go out with him again, even though no date with him would ever be the kind of date a girl dreamed about. Homer would always do and say unexpected, disconcerting things, but that was the kind of boy he was. And a girl would not have to analyze every remark, every quirk of his eyebrow, when she went out with a boy like Homer. She would not have to wonder if he liked her just a shade less than he had the day before if he happened to say, Hi, instead of Hi, Jean.

Jean was still sitting on the bed tenderly massaging her foot when she heard a car stop in front of the house, and in a few minutes the front door opened and Sue tiptoed down the hall.

"Hello," whispered Jean.

"Hi," answered Sue, silently closing the door. "Did you have fun?"

"Yes and no," answered Jean. "Mostly yes. Did you?"

"Oh, yes," sighed Sue, and dropped down on her own bed. "I had a wonderful time. Just wonderful. We saw *The Great Train Robbery* and some old Chaplin comedies."

Jean thought she had never seen her sister look so pretty, and she knew that prettiness was not caused by old movies. Jean rose from the bed and walked gingerly to the closet. She wished she were floating on a cloud like Sue—then her feet might not hurt so much. She removed her coat and as she did so, she put her hand in her pocket and took out the paper covering from the straw. She hung her coat in the closet, but instead of throwing the straw covering into the wastebasket, she smoothed it out and read the words printed on it. *Sani-straw. Pat. U.S. Off.*

"You know something?" said Sue dreamily.

"What?" asked Jean, absently winding the flattened paper tube around her finger.

"Ken kissed me good night," whispered Sue.

Jean looked curiously at her sister, radiant because Ken had kissed her. It must be a lovely feeling. "I guess Ken changed a lot as he grew up," she reflected.

"Mm-hm." Sue slipped off her coat and kicked off

her shoes. "A whole lot. He makes the boys at school seem childish."

"Sue, how did you feel that day you ran into Ken at the library?" Jean asked.

"Oh, I don't know. Surprised that he had changed so much, and not sure what to say to him." Sue pulled her dress off over her head.

"You didn't feel all full of pinwheels at the sight of him?" persisted Jean.

"Pinwheels and Fourth of July sparklers? Of course not, silly. I just thought he had turned out to be an awfully nice boy," said Sue.

"Do you think you would have liked him as much if you had gone out with him two years ago?" There was so much Jean wanted to know.

"You are certainly full of questions tonight," answered Sue. "No, I don't think I would have liked him very much two years ago. He wouldn't have grown up enough. And now if you want first turn at the bathroom you had better stop playing with that piece of paper, and get started."

"You go first," said Jean, still toying with the wrapper from the straw. Maybe that was what a lot of girls should do—all they could do, really—wait for the boys to grow up. And in the meantime there were other things to do . . . the things she and Elaine had always enjoyed doing together . . . and now there was Homer and his flock of pigeons.

Jean decided she really would keep the straw wrapper for a souvenir. She opened her top drawer and took out a Japanese lacquered box, which held the odds and ends she did not quite know what to do with, but still did not want to throw away: her junior-high school graduation diploma, a paper napkin from a birthday party, a ball-point pen that needed a refill. As she removed the box from the drawer, her eye fell on the snapshot of Johnny which she had thrown into the drawer and half forgotten about. Now she picked it up and studied it critically. How charming he looked smiling into the camera, and how miserable she looked facing Johnny and trying to peek at the camera at the same time! All that was behind her now. The real Johnny would always do what Johnny wanted and never mind how other people felt. The Johnny she had admired was no more real than Kip Laddish on the television screen.

Jean started to tear the snapshot in two, hesitated, and looked at it a second time. Johnny, the boy she neither liked nor admired, and yet . . . she would never forget Johnny. It was Johnny who had noticed her, singled her out of the crowd, had made her feel that she was attractive. In a way, it was Johnny who had made her aware of herself. She could not forget that. If only Johnny had been a different kind of boy. . . .

Jean picked up a pair of manicure scissors from the dresser and carefully snipped off her half of the snapshot and dropped it into the wastebasket. She lifted the lid of the lacquered box and dropped into it the wrapper of the straw. Her glance lingered on Johnny's half of the snapshot, which she laid on top of the wrapper. Silently she closed the box and shut it in her drawer. Good-by, Johnny, she thought. I am not sorry I knew you. Maybe she should be sorry, but she wasn't. In her heart she knew she would remember Johnny. Always.